Crossroads

D. A. Spruzen

Two Novellas

ISBN 978-0-9859628-2-1

E-book ISBN 978-0-9859628-3-8

Cover design and interior formatting by Melanie Stephens with MSIllustration and Design.

Cover photo credit Peter Hellebrand.

Printing by Createspace.

For my brothers,
Michael and David Spruzen.

Contents

*At every crossroads on the path that leads to the future, tradition
has placed 10,000 men to guard the past.*

— Maurice Maeterlinck

Crossroads

1
George

Floating now, he cannot tear away from Pamela's hard glassy eyes, more like blue and white marbles than anything human. He feels the tide sucking him back out and digs his fingers into the wet sand, but cannot gain purchase. Her eyes begin to undulate, and behind a sheer curtain of water their hues mutate as he drifts further away. He comes up for breath whenever the current releases him from its clutching and snatching, but soon it increases its grip with inexorable force. He closes his eyes as he fights to put off taking a breath. His lungs are spent, he hears his last intake—not of air, but of tepid, salty water—and feels the relief of it, the searing pain of it. He opens his eyes once more and sees those eyes fading and pulling back and up into the waves that crash over his head.

She let him go, never reached out a hand to pull him back.

She'd stopped loving him when he came back broken.

Freedom now, a bitter freedom.

Swept far away into old dreams, he surrenders to the warmth of it, the lightness of it.

2
Sophie

I wasn't sure I could find the farm again. It is so changed I nearly missed it—additions and improvements, and a neat arid garden in the style of all English gardens here, sad plants sown in soils and climates that reject them wholeheartedly. They bought all my land, but there are other houses now, so they must have sold some off. There is no one left who would remember I ever lived in that house. I never told Tom or Julian.

I am drawn to the little grave. Let me sit awhile. Let me see if remembrance presses too hard, grabs at my breath and soul, needs holding at bay with busyness and charade.

Claude, my husband, once. My silly girlish fascination with him started me down this path. I met him while he was waiting tables in a London restaurant. He was uneducated and unpolished, but his charming French accent and mannerisms blinded me to his flaws, although my parents saw through him. For the first time I saw Dad out of control as he ranted about "that damned foreigner," and "throwing herself away on a nobody." The day after a big row, I sat in the kitchen, watching Dad with contempt, I'm ashamed to say, as he went about his usual morning routine. He sat hunched over the table mangling his newspaper, excoriating the "they" of the government with the same old belabored complaints, all the while quaffing strong cups of tea while he waited for Mother to serve his bacon and eggs. Their days were crammed with little rituals that rendered their lives devoid of meaning, at least in my youthful judgment. They coasted along year after year over, what had been until then, an untroubled surface of platitudes and routines. I, on the other hand, was on my way to new adventures with an exotic young man who would show me the world beyond dull English suburbia.

Poor things, they got along the only way they knew, made the best of their lives, and loved their daughter. They had always distrusted the unknown and were no doubt prejudiced, but perhaps they did perceive the baseness of Claude's nature that my love-misted eyes overlooked.

We were married in the local registry office as Father declared that inviting our friends to a proper wedding was out of the question, and a wicked waste of money besides. Claude's father died six months later. He insisted on moving back to take care of the family farm in the Languedoc, raising sheep for the milk needed by local cheese-makers. I had realized my mistake by then but, already pregnant, had little choice. Mother and Father waved goodbye with red-rimmed dry eyes and clenched lips. Heartless, I felt only irritation. As their only child I had denied them the satisfaction of hosting a pretty wedding and becoming grandparents to another generation of British middle-class rectitude. I resented them too much at the time to care for their sorrow, although when I crossed the threshold of that old farmhouse for the first time, homesickness punched the breath out of me.

The little stone house was dank and murky, permeated by more than a century's odors of cooking and stale armpits. One large room downstairs served as kitchen and living room, and I discovered two small bedrooms up a worn flight of narrow stairs. Ten minutes after I arrived, Claude's gorgon of a mother made a dramatic departure to live with her sister on the grounds that she could hardly be expected to share her kitchen with a foreigner. I went upstairs to unpack and wash my hands, but couldn't find the bathroom. Since the outhouse is no longer there, I have to assume that situation has been rectified. I think it was where that greenhouse sits now. I had never lived without indoor plumbing and a proper kitchen. I looked around me then with clear eyes and mind—at the house, out of the few cloudy windows, then at my scruffy and sulky husband—and realized how far I had mired myself in poverty and misery.

I had no idea how to cook over a fire, which infuriated Claude that first day. I lost my temper, yelling that since I hadn't been brought up in a hovel, I could hardly be expected to know how to live in one. He slapped my face. I ran upstairs, dived under the poor thin blankets, and closed my eyes. I heard him come up hours later, cursing in a drunken fury. I held my breath, but he flopped down in the other room and was soon snoring. In the morning I told him to keep out of my bed for the safety of the baby and he agreed. Selfish and boorish as he was in lust, he wanted a son. We hardly spoke after that, although he berated me from time to time for my many inadequacies.

I would look at him while he shoveled food into his mouth and wonder what I could have seen in him. I used to think him good looking with his sharp features and thick smudgy-black hair. But he wasn't good looking any more because his face had assumed a somewhat feral look now he was back in his natural setting. I no longer found any flirtatious sparkle in his eyes, only the occasional glitter of contempt. The supple soft hands that used to caress me were callused now and rarely clean. He smelled like the animals he bred. I suppose he hadn't really changed, just reverted.

I gradually gained some mastery over that stove, although I didn't know any of the recipes his mother had brought him up to crave. Often, I would make dinner and he would go to his mother's house to eat without telling me. He never invited me to go along, and when he got back, would smirk as he remarked on the wonderful meal he had just enjoyed. All I wanted to do was to survive from one day to the next. It would have been the beginning of insanity to think of the future. I did hide some money away, though. Claude hadn't noticed my father pushing the notes into my coat pocket when I left. I could see a time when I would have to escape back to England with my child— for the little one's sake as much as mine.

I labored alone on the lumpy bed while a punishing storm lashed the house. Claude stayed out in the barn, tending a birthing ewe that was in some difficulty. He said that since this was my first, I had a long way to go and he'd fetch the doctor when he could. The ewe and her twin lambs survived, but my baby did not. Poor little boy, I don't think he drew more than a few breaths. The doctor might have saved him. As it was, he arrived after it was all over and told me I would never again bear a child. We had no telephone, so I asked him to book a taxi for the day of the funeral as I needed to go home to see my parents. He quite understood.

I packed one suitcase—I couldn't carry more. Claude must have noticed but said nothing. He tucked the tiny coffin he'd made under one arm, like he did the lambs he sometimes took to slaughter. That offended me on some deep level. I told him to show some respect and use both hands, as if bearing an offering. I expected him to ignore me, but he did it without commenting or even looking my way.

I stood on one side of the open grave and Claude slouched sullenly on the other as we watched our son being lowered into the crumbly earth. My mother-in-law stood at some distance clasping her hands in prayer, looking grim and triumphant. After the priest had finished his mumbling, I walked away, each thud of dirt on the coffin plucking at my nerves. I knew without looking that my mother-in-law had taken my place at the graveside.

I picked up the suitcase I'd left leaning against the church gate and got into the waiting taxi for the ride down the mountains and into Montpellier.

3
Julian

I just want to be left alone for a bit, see if I can dredge up some happy memories to take my mind off things. Thank God for my study. It's down an old passageway, the one place guests can't find me, the only place where I can lock the door and be still. Even Sophie never comes here.

What a balls-up. What an absolute bloody disaster. Two deaths in as many days, and two widows. I should never have invited them, or at least told Tom and George what I'd done. I thought it would be interesting, amusing to see how these two behaved after all this time—over thirty-five years now.

The old brain gets a bit fidgety sometimes. I've got a good library here, but it's not easy to buy new English-language books. I speak French well enough, but I don't much enjoy reading it. Too much like schoolwork. I kept most of my classics and I still enjoy dipping into the Aeneid from time to time, but I taught those texts for so long they're pretty much played out for me. Chucked out Gallic Wars, who the hell needs to know all those words for different kinds of fortifications? Crashing bore. When even the teacher is bored, it's a hard road to keep the class up to scratch. Catullus has his moments, of course, but you can't do much of that with teenagers. Down in Montpellier, you mostly find silly romances for English tourists; that's too far in the other direction.

I like having the inn, but I miss teaching sometimes. Not that drilling Latin declensions into teenage brains is particularly taxing, but we used to have some fair old discussions in the common room. We did think things through a lot, philosophical questions, that sort of thing. Perhaps I should sell up. But what then? I'm devilish fond of Sophie, and I'm used to the life now. Going down to the coast for the day and soaking up a bit of sun is pleasant. We do get sunny weather up here, just not so often and not so warm. It's beautiful, too, and I've built up the business quite nicely. No, it's only the guilt nagging. Not that I did anything wrong, I was just the catalyst that set these unfortunate events in motion. I couldn't possibly have known how it would all turn out.

I'd often thought about the war and the time Tom, George and I were wounded. I was curious to see what sort of man George had become. He behaved very badly, but people can change and grow as they age. The whole sorry incident shocked me given his father's military record, but I suppose he was the proverbial black sheep. I once started to tell Sophie something of the story and was surprised to find that Tom had already told her. I knew they'd been lovers, but assumed Tom would never mention the subject to anyone. I have to admit to feeling a little pang over the intimacy this revelation implied. Well, if the classics have taught me one thing, it's that jealousy is a monster to be cast out of mind at first appearance. Sophie and I are still together, and that's what matters.

To mere acquaintances, Tom was the kind of man whose name you would have to be reminded of each time you ran into him. I can't imagine what Sophie would have seen in him. Better than nothing, I suppose, and whom could she have met teaching at a girls' boarding school? I knew he'd become a successful barrister and wondered how good living and success might have changed him. Had he become fat and pompous, perhaps? He hadn't, he was just the same quiet, steady chap whom clients must have found reassuring. I always heard from both George and Tom at Christmas, but I knew they would never have contacted each other.

Maybe it was a touch malicious on my part, but I think it was mostly curiosity that inspired me to arrange the reunion. After talking it over with Sophie, I decided to close the inn for a week in mid-September, after most of the holidaymakers had left. Actually, Sophie was eager to see Tom and George, too, so she shouldn't put all the blame on me.

I watched them all as they arrived, how they responded to each other, how they scrutinized each other. They tried to be surreptitious after the initial encounter, but I noted all the little glances. And so did George's wife, Pamela. Daphne was oblivious to anything but her own spot on the social canvas.

Fascinating.

Pamela and George arrived first, George—shockingly deteriorated—grumbled and complained as he was helped out of the car into his wheelchair. Thank heavens I'd installed a ramp to the main level for my older guests. I greeted them and led them into the sitting room where Sophie was waiting. George started when he saw her, recognized her at once. Perhaps she was still the heroine of his nighttime fantasies. Looking at him, fantasies would be about all he had left. She walked over and kissed him on the cheek.

"Hello, George, sorry to see you're in a wheel chair. How are you? It's so nice to see you again. And you must be Pamela."

"Hello, Sophie, I wasn't expecting to see you. I thought it was just Pamela and me." George's voice sounded reedy, none too steady.

Pamela said nothing, just watched George as he gazed at Sophie. He was too shaken to pretend indifference.

"Oh, no, Tom and Daphne are coming, too. It'll be quite the reunion," I said in my jolliest voice.

George drew a sharp breath at that revelation and I'm afraid he saw I was amused by his discomfiture. When we heard the other car pull up his color heightened and sweat beaded his forehead. Tom's eyes widened when he saw Sophie beside me, but narrowed as he understood our relationship almost at once. The room was full of undercurrents by this time, and even I felt a bit off-kilter.

Daphne swept into the room behind her husband and made her rounds. A social climber in blinders, she clearly noticed nothing untoward—no tension, no pairs of eyes tracking Sophie, not even George's nervous watchfulness. She acknowledged each guest according to the slot she allotted them: Pamela as eminently suitable, George as a war hero (the bugger actually apologized for not getting up due to his war wound!), and me as the distinguished intellectual she assumed a classics master must be; Sophie, hard to place in her circumscribed register, merited only a perfunctory greeting. George watched Tom much as a mouse watches a snake.

The women are strikingly different. Daphne, perhaps ten years younger than the rest of us, is not so much well-preserved as aggressively impeccable. She has a thin hard mouth, which her bright red lipstick does nothing to soften. Pamela, like many of her class, dresses in casual, sometimes sloppy clothes that nevertheless offer an overall effect of style. She is quietly self-assured and understated— except for that surprising black hair. Nothing else stands out, but the overall effect is pleasing. You can tell there's plenty of solid muscle under those baggy clothes. As far as Pamela is concerned, those who matter know who and what she is, and she doesn't give a damn for anyone else's opinion. Daphne's type can never enjoy that social ease and, to her, appearances would be everything. Sophie, by contrast, enjoys a simple elegance that she seems to have absorbed from the French, a subtlety quite beyond Daphne's ken or Pamela's interest.

Sophie hasn't said much since Tom and George died, and probably blames me. Of course, she is probably quite sad; she and Tom were once lovers after all, albeit long ago. And I suppose she had a very brief interlude with George in hospital, as she did with all of us. What a wonderful girl she was, so compassionate and sweet. We all loved her. We didn't think of her as cheap. You think differently about things like that in wartime.

She was a terrific nurse—tender and loving, firm when necessary, and steel-tough when she had to be. She told me later that she believed the souls of shattered boys and men must also be nursed if their broken bodies are to heal. When Sophie gave us our sponge baths, her soapy hands would caress us gently and intimately. From those of us who were regaining our strength, one day there would be a sudden intake of breath and our eyes, no doubt full of need, would catch hers, and we knew our turn would come soon. The whispers went up and down the lines of beds in the wards, so the men all knew the drill. On an evening when Sophie was on night duty, one of us lucky fellows might receive a visit, the curtains around his bed would be drawn, and, if the moon were generous, her faint silhouette could be seen dispensing her healing balms. Men lucky enough to have an intact hand would find it slipping under the covers. When she drew back the curtains as briskly as if all she had been doing was lancing a boil, a collective sigh of relief would go up from those who were still awake and paying attention.

There was poetry in her tenderness, so I decided to write a poem about her after I was deemed fit to return to duty. I used to think it through after I was sent back to the lines, think up lofty phrases as I lay on my bunk trying not to wonder what morning might bring—shattering pain, or perhaps oblivion; or, if I were lucky, just another sleepless night. But everything I came up with sounded trite. I even tried Latin, but that sounded clumsy. Nothing about Sophie was ever clumsy. I gave up after a few weeks. Anyway, you could hardly bandy that sort of thing around, not in those days. Too many people would have put two and two together.

We thought no less of Nurse Sophie for those attentions so freely given, for we recognized the depth of her compassion. In another time and place we would have bristled at any display of pity or sympathy, but for the moment we felt differently. We adored her. We respected her. I noticed she always made herself scarce when our families came to visit. I expect she was afraid the yearning in some of the fellows' eyes might arouse suspicion. Innate tact, that's Sophie all over.

When we were well enough, we'd be allowed to walk around Hastings and come back to a different ward to sleep. Sometimes those of us who could afford it would take Sophie out to dinner, expecting nothing in return. Tom and I took her out several times. Most of us were a little in love with her, although her invariable sweetness of manner revealed nothing of herself, almost as if she'd covered her emotions with a sheet and stored them in the attic for the time being.

George Laster was a patient in the same hospital, but was too badly wounded to get out of bed. I spotted Sophie enter his room quite stealthily one night, though, so she must have been able to comfort him in ways that accommodated his smashed hip. Sophie once asked Tom and me why we never visited George. She just shrugged at our noncommittal grunts. She knew better than to press.

After a few weeks, George was moved to a larger hospital for further surgery and Tom and I were sent back to fight in the hell that was wartime France.

At war's end, I was content to resume my post as classics master at Beeston Hall. The petty irritations of school life did nothing to disturb my gratitude for its relative serenity after the horrors I'd seen at the front. We spent our summer holidays at the country house I inherited from my father and I loved those breaks, even though Janet was always rather a wet blanket at best.

I was delighted when Sophie telephoned me. I think I sounded too delighted, because Janet stared at me with those slitty eyes she used to get when she looked at boys who slopped their tea into saucers. She always insisted on having groups of boys round for tea, and then got cross when they were less than

21

dainty. School housing was comfortable, but pretty shabby, so I don't know what all the fuss was about. Oh well, mustn't speak ill of the dead. Janet was a good wife and mother, God rest her soul.

At any rate, I'm glad I was the one to answer the phone. "Major Stephens? This is Sophie James from the hospital in Hastings. I nursed you after you were wounded. Do you remember me?"

That voice, that light charm. "Sister Sophie, how simply splendid to hear from you. What are you doing now?"

"Call me Sophie, please. I was demobbed last week. I don't quite know what to do next. I just found out my parents' house was bombed and they were both killed. I wanted to ask your advice, because I don't want to nurse any more."

"You just come and stay with us in the country for a bit. My wife, Janet—you'll like her—will make you very welcome. A spot of fresh air and some good meals will do you good. Then we can put our heads together."

She sounded down and lost, quite lacking the crisp demeanor I remembered. I was glad to help, but Janet needed some persuading. I explained that Sister Sophie had displayed a selfless devotion toward all her patients and deserved their gratitude, which was true enough.

When she thought I wasn't looking, Janet's eyes iced over and watched Sophie as if she were a wasp at a picnic. Janet watched me, too, and I had to be careful not to be too chummy, at least when she was around. She was eager to help Sophie find a job—eager to get rid of her, I'd say—but it was I who found her a post teaching French at a girls' boarding school not far from our place. The headmistress said she was delighted to have found such a refined candidate, one who spoke French fluently and had served her country with distinction. And who was English. She said she'd never been comfortable with native

French teachers, who seemed to have a different way of looking at life, an outlook that was not sufficiently British to be entrusted with impressionable young minds. If she'd only known!

Sophie visited us for a couple of weeks each summer for years, an event that was anticipated eagerly by me, although not by Janet, of course. She'd purse her lips and sigh like a martyr when the time came. The tension level was practically buzzing by the time fair Sophie came into sight, striding out of the station with her portmanteau. And she was indeed fair, with her curly light brown hair, flawless skin, blue eyes and a taut figure that spoke of many bracing country walks with a bevy of schoolgirls. And the remarkable thing is, she doesn't look much different to me now than she did then.

The visits went on until Sophie retired to Montpellier. I went over a couple of times while Janet was off visiting her mother. Of course, I was given the silent treatment for a few weeks after each trip. We went to visit her together once, against Janet's strenuous objections. I'd told her I didn't mind going alone, but that didn't suit her, either, although it would have suited me just fine.

Sophie told us a friend owned an inn up in the Cevennes and we should drive up there and spend a couple of nights. It only took about two and a half hours, and the scenery was marvelous. That was all it took.

It's an ancient place, all of stone, even the roof and chimney as is common in the Languedoc. The ceilings in the upper rooms are gracefully arched to spread the tremendous load. I love the solitude, the sensual pleasure of emerging from chilled stone into warm sunshine, and the relaxed chatter of summer guests, so uplifting after the clipped monotones of too many cloistered years. We had a wonderful time; well, I did. Our host told me he was going to sell up the following year and retire to his daughter's house in Provence. My French was good even then, so Janet had no idea what we were talking about because she didn't believe in foreign languages. Or foreigners.

We explored timing, price, and everything else. I would turn sixty at about the time he wanted to sell, and I'd already decided that the next year would be my last at Beeston Hall. After we returned home, I thought of little else.

Janet was so stunned when I told her the deal was done, that she said nothing. In fact, come to think of it, she spoke to me even less than before after that evening I told her we were moving. I confess I was often impatient with her after we got here as she always seemed tired and dispirited. She never tried to learn French, thought they were a decadent lot. She complained that the cool and windy climate in the mountains didn't suit her, and acted sickly more often than not. Tedious. We didn't realize until too late that the real problem was that she had cancer and would die within the year. I had been quite fond of her and was sorry for her suffering. I missed and mourned her for several months.

I was glad of Sophie's companionship—still am. She's remained youthful and I'm upright and fit, and she's sensible enough to stay out of the way when my children visit with their families. I hope she stays with me. I seem to love her. I'm not sure I've ever felt real love for a woman before. Funny thing to happen at my time of life. My parents liked Janet and she seemed the right sort at the time, and to be honest, all I'd felt for all the other girls I'd asked out was straightforward lust. I'd feel absolutely rotten if Sophie left me.

Just my luck if cook gives us all food poisoning tonight— tie up all the loose ends, so to speak. Hope this cock-up doesn't make it into the papers.

4
Sophie

I couldn't bring myself to return to my parents' tight-lipped vindication after I left Claude—I'd have had to admit they were right—so I tried my luck in Montpellier where I managed to find a job teaching English at a small private school that provided housing. What a beautiful little oasis it was; remembering the affectionate camaraderie of both teachers and students still brings a smile to my face. But, war interrupted. After France surrendered to Germany, the south was still relatively unfettered, so I was able to find my way back to England. To my everlasting regret, I was still unwilling to see my parents, so I joined the Army Nurse Corps. As the butchery wound on, I became an accredited nurse, learning my craft the hardest way possible.

I was redeployed to Sicily after a ghastly, harrowing journey that made the London Blitz seem peaceful. A steady diet of landmines and strafing eats deep into your mind. I still can't stand loud or sudden noises, even a popping balloon. After that we were sent into Germany for the final push in 1945. I had nursed the most appallingly wounded men almost from the start of my career, but I ended the war caring for concentration camp victims liberated from Dachau, a haunting assignment. They always walk with me, those empty-eyed stick people, peace forever beyond their reach.

I returned to England in 1946, sick at heart now I could allow myself to acknowledge the brutality visited on and by my patients through those years. Men are hopeless, always ready to mete out destruction to those who challenge their politics, religion, possession, or love. I vowed I would never again nurse or marry.

Finally, I steeled myself to visit my parents. I walked up the street to find a weedy bombsite that used to be my home and no trace of my parents, who were destroyed along with it. The notification never got through.

Death seemed to haunt my every breath, sleeping or waking. I walked back to the station and sat through the journey in a daze as the train dragged me back to London. After picking at a paltry meal at Lyon's Corner House—we were still on wartime rations—I wandered into a small park and sat on a bench, wondering what to do next. Then I remembered Julian. I still had his address, so I rang him to ask his advice. He asked me down to stay for a few weeks. He was really sweet, although I don't think his wife liked me much. Janet was a dour creature. Julian found out about the job teaching French at a private school for girls through an old friend, and off I went.

I gave the headmistress an edited version of my background to explain how I came to speak French so well. I told her my husband had died shortly after we moved to France and that I had taught English at a private school. I did not acknowledge my dead son, even to myself. I think it's time I tried to open my heart to him. Is it too late to be a mother? I've never felt like a mother. I'll wait awhile.

Masefield School for Young Ladies was a stodgy establishment, not as happy a place as the one in Montpellier. I would have gone back to France, but when I got in touch with one of the teachers who still lived in the town, I discovered the school had closed down when the Germans took it over for officers' quarters.

5
Tom

The landscape was absolutely magnificent, so he didn't mind taking George for a spin. Mountains and rough terrain. Unspoiled. Just the sort of place Daphne hated. He would never have spilled any secrets back there, but George wasn't to know that. He shouldn't have rattled his chain, wasn't quite the thing given what a sorry specimen the man had become. Tom almost felt sorry for him, but had no wish to talk to him, not that he'd opened his mouth since they'd set out, thank God.

Lovely seeing Sophie again, even though she lived with Julian now, lucky blighter. Could she possibly love him? Wonderful girl. Too bad she turned him down when he'd asked her to marry him back in '47, just after she went to teach at that ghastly boarding school. Told him she wasn't ready and couldn't possibly think of settling down after all she'd seen. Said she had these dreams, terrible nightmares.

He had his own nightmares, all kinds, but the worst one, the one that came most often, found him lying bleeding under a tree, helpless as a German soldier rammed his Luger against Tom's head. The icy metal burned into his temple until the pain propelled him into fearful wakefulness. Something like what could have happened the day George deserted him.

He fancied he could picture every tree in that clearing, every chiseled stone in that old henhouse. Impossible, he supposed, but his mind's snapshot images looked as sharp as anything he saw in front of him now. The three of them got cut off from their unit in Italy after a hard battle. So many had died, and such hard deaths. He could hear his own rasping breaths as they dodged around trees and rocks, bent almost double as they tried to outrun their German pursuers. They came to an abandoned farmhouse on the edge of some woods. With the temperature dropping, thunder rumbling, George wanted to take shelter. He sulked when they overruled him, but they couldn't risk getting trapped.

Tom had taken a bullet in his shoulder—the left one fortunately—and stopped to rest in a little copse they found within sight of the house. He'd lost a lot of blood, and needed to keep pressure on the wound. Julian's thigh was torn up by shrapnel and he decided to carry on moving back as long as he could, so Tom told him to go ahead, they'd catch up. Julian and Tom had left a fairly obvious trail of blood, so he didn't hold out much hope. George wasn't wounded. Strange he didn't go with Julian.

Tom closed his eyes for a few minutes, the memories still so raw.

"Tom. Tom!"

He must have stopped walking. "George! Sorry. Miles away."

"What were you going to say back there?"

"Nothing. Nothing at all. It was all a long time ago."

"I don't believe you. You want revenge. I know you do."

"Never mind, George, never mind. What does it matter after all this time?"

George looked rigid from the back, his head hung low, shoulders raised and hunched. Tom kept on walking.

He'd closed his eyes for a few minutes in that copse, too. The place was a little Eden, bucolic and unspoiled. It felt wonderful at first, but when you've been under attack for so long, peace and quiet can suddenly acquire a threatening ambiance. Too much quiet, no birdsong, a twig snaps, and paranoia hits. He'd snapped open his eyes, and realized George had left him. He saw the back of him disappearing into a stone henhouse and spotted a glint of metal through a chink in the wall.

The chickens, disturbed and angry, gave him away. One German burst into the henhouse with the second close behind, and they were killed immediately, but George didn't let up, just went on shooting wildly. Tom remembered being so angry, thinking what a silly ass he was to waste ammunition like that. He didn't think of being angry because George abandoned him until later. He saw George duck out of the back of the coop and bolt behind the farmhouse. One of the Germans threw a grenade into the henhouse, and another lobbed one into the farmhouse, probably thinking they faced many more soldiers than just two. It looked as if there were only three Germans left standing, so Tom crawled closer and tossed a grenade right at them. Blew them to smithereens. Terrible what war does to a man. That horrible mangled mess hadn't bothered him at all. He'd scored a goal for the home team.

"What became of you after the war?"

"I'm a barrister. I became senior partner after my father retired."

"You always were a bit of a pompous ass. Suppose it's almost a requirement in your profession. Children?"

"Two. James is in his last year at the Royal Academy of Music, although goodness knows where that will get him. Daphne was furious. She wanted him to attain the sort of position in society I supposedly enjoy. I backed him up though,

I want him to be happy. Believe it or not, I never wanted to be a pompous ass."

George gave a contemptuous wave of his hand. Tom was glad he couldn't see that weasel face.

"Ellen went to teacher's training college. We have a house just outside Oxford, the sort of house a man like me is supposed to have. An appropriate house, as my wife would say. There's a man Daphne found who makes our garden the envy of our avenue, at least since our dog obliged her by dying last year—he kept digging up the herbaceous borders. She hates dogs, complains they're mucky things, but the children and I always insisted on having one. I've had a good life by most measures, and I've been miserable for most of it."

"What do you think mine's been like living with Madam Bossyboots?"

"We all dig our own holes, George." George twisted around then, his expression venomous, eyes wandering over Tom as if unable to find a landing place.

"Why are you taunting me? Are you trying to shame me?"

Tom kept moving, the ground sloping higher now, the wheelchair heavier with every step.

He'd waited for a few minutes, but nothing moved. They must have become separated from their unit, too. He managed to crawl behind the house and discovered George bleeding badly from a hip wound. Tom bandaged him up as best he could with his own shirt. When he'd asked him why he'd hidden in the henhouse, he replied he could see no point in both of them dying. After all, Tom was already wounded and giving their position away with his blood trail. He hadn't glossed over the fact that he'd abandoned his comrade to save himself. Tom half dragged and half carried him until they caught up with Julian. In spite of his own wound, Julian helped with George and the three of them somehow made it back to their line. A field hospital nurse patched them up and put them on a convoy that started the dangerous evacuation back to England. Not everyone survived the bumpy, painful journey and the occasional strafing, but the three of them made it to Sophie's hospital in Hastings.

And here they were, thirty-five years later, with George in a wheelchair, at Tom's mercy. What kind of a melodramatic thought was that? Tom's armpits grew sticky as rage clouded his mind.

"You do know I did the only logical thing, don't you?"

"And I know I didn't. The logical thing would have been to leave you behind to bleed to death and concentrate on saving myself."

"Did you tell any of them?"

"No," he lied. He could see George's shoulders hunching closer and closer to his ears, and his voice had taken on a curious warble. He'd told Julian the story one night when he got drunk after learning George was to be decorated for gallantry.

"This is a pretty spot, George, I'll brake your chair a little away from the edge, but you'll still be able to see the river."

"Park it over there, under a tree. I've got to take a leak. I can get up and do that on my own, so keep your distance."

Tom left him there and walked to the edge of the cliff. The River Tarn's untamed power, its roar muffled by distance, disconcerted him, seemed to call.

He'd told Sophie, too. They had become lovers after the war, but she said she would never marry and he'd wanted children at the time. Daphne was his father's secretary, and had seemed a sweet and accommodating little thing—until they got married. Tom loved both his children, but considered them spoiled, always had an eye for the main chance, just like their mother. His fault too, he supposed. He'd taken the easier road with them too often. He hated confrontation in private life, although he relished it in the courtroom. He was an actor who donned a role along with his wig and robes, a role that freed him to execute his usual devastating performance in court; let's face it, act the bully.

About five years into the marriage, he'd run into Sophie at the Tate. They both loved art, and Tom reveled in the gallery's church quiet. They became lovers again almost immediately, meeting whenever they could get away. She relished staying in a nice hotel and eating decent food for a change. Tom liked to treat her to something new to wear sometimes, and loved seeing her pleasure in a pretty frock or blouse.

He drove down to pick her up at school once, pretending to be her cousin. The headmistress who came to inspect him, a frightening, whiskered woman, had marched down a sludge brown hallway toward him like an avenging angel. After they'd made their getaway, he asked Sophie how she could stand living in such a drab place. She agreed it was dreary, especially compared with the school she taught at in Montpellier before the war, but said the tedium was mostly welcome after the dreadful things she'd seen. He'd had no idea she'd lived in France, she'd never mentioned it before. But she clenched her teeth as if she didn't want to talk about it. Tom understood he shouldn't pursue it.

He'd felt pretty devastated when she moved to Montpellier. He went over every couple of months, and Daphne didn't seem surprised to hear he suddenly had business in France. Probably glad to get rid of him for a time. All in all, they were lovers for nearly thirty years. He'd never tired of her; she always sparkled for him, was always refreshing, rejuvenating.

He remembered that afternoon when they lay on her bed enjoying the warm breeze that drifted through the open windows.

After a few minutes, she sat up and poured some wine. He held up his glass and looked through it at her breasts, admiring them through its rosy hue as they undulated with her every movement.

"Tom, you never mention George, although Julian keeps me up-to-date. He's always very negative about him. What is it between the three of you? I found it so strange that neither of you visited him when he was bedridden, and once I saw you and him having quite a tiff."

Taken aback—they never discussed that terrible time—he set down his glass and turned to look at her.

"All right, I'll tell you the story, because I know I can rely on your discretion."

"I won't tell anyone."

He remembered Sophie's unwavering gaze as he talked. He knew she'd had some hair-raising moments of her own during the war, had experienced the fear of imminent death.

"He just left you to their mercy?"

"He did." He thought, hoped, he saw love in her eyes then.

"You were the real hero, Tom."

"I don't know about me being a hero, but he certainly wasn't. And don't forget Julian helped too. When George was well enough to talk, I tackled him about his behavior, and this must have been the exchange you noticed. George told me to keep my mouth shut, it was my word against his, and I couldn't prove anything. And he was right, I couldn't. After that, he wouldn't speak to me or look at me."

"Ashamed of himself, do you think?"

"I don't know if he's capable of shame. He's too keen on flaunting his medal, one of those types who like to pretend a substance they don't have. Lots of chaps lost their nerve sometimes, and it's not something you'd report usually. But they didn't masquerade as heroes. That's the shame of it."

"And he was pretty cold-blooded about his reasons, too," Sophie murmured as she stroked his neck. "Of course, pain and

D.A. SPRUZEN

fear tends to make people reveal themselves. I've heard the most incredible outpourings in my time."

Tom had closed his eyes and leaned back, surprised that reliving the ordeal had distressed him so much. It had been more than thirty years, after all.

"Sophie, if I can get a divorce from Daphne, would you marry me? I've always loved you, you know."

"Oh, Tom, I wouldn't feel right about breaking up a home."

"Our home was broken long ago."

She took him into her arms again and they slept.

Tom inhaled, remembering the scent of her skin. She always carried a faint aroma of spring flowers. He must kiss her again, on the cheek, only to see if she still smelled the same. Could he win her back? Was that a mad idea, was he losing his grip, was he really willing to act like a cad? She'd looked at him once or twice in a way that let him know she remembered. If he could get her back he'd love her for ever, Julian and Daphne be damned. He had to get back to the inn, to her.

George grunted and Tom turned to see him standing at a tree, legs bowed like an old man, piddling like a puppy. A sudden gust of wind threw a fine spray of urine over his trousers. George growled something inaudible, and noticed Tom looking.

"Fuck off!" he screeched.

Tom turned away, suppressing an absurd impulse to laugh as he remembered some American flyboys he'd met in a bar in Soho. Those Yanks employed some marvelous epithets, and "go piss in the wind" had been one of his favorites.

The day he got home from that trip, he'd called Daphne into his study and told her there was someone else and he wanted a divorce.

"Our marriage ended long ago, Daphne. You don't love me any more, admit it."

"You bloody bastard. That's not the point, is it, after all these years? It's never the same when you're not part of a couple anymore, you lose your place in society. You have to keep up appearances, no matter what." She'd wrapped her arms around herself as if to hold everything in.

"No, I won't give you a bloody divorce, not if you know what's good for you. Do you think people trust a barrister who keeps a fancy woman? And I'll make sure they all hear about it. And what of your children? What do you think they'll have to say? They'll hate you! And what about your father?"

Her voice had risen, sharp and steely now, and her fists settled on her hips. Tom watched her, paralyzed, as his hopes slipped out of reach.

And that had been the end of it. He'd written to Sophie and told her he couldn't marry her, told her what Daphne said. They met a few more times and never mentioned marriage again. A couple of years later she'd written a gentle letter, telling him there was someone else. Tom wrote back, wishing her happiness, always.

He banished Sophie from his mind after that, couldn't bear thinking of the happiness he'd missed out on. He'd managed to keep the anguish at bay these past five years. Until he'd walked into the inn and saw her next to Julian.

"I have nothing to be ashamed of, or are you sorry I saved your life, shot those Nazi bastards?"

He hadn't heard George come up behind him. Damn him, interrupting his reverie with ugly griping.

"You left me to die, George, and it was I who wiped out the last of them. And I hold you in utter contempt."

"How dare you! And you have no proof, remember that. I will destroy you in the courts if you mention a word of this slander."

"Not slander, George, the truth. And you deserve to have people know you for the sniveling coward you are. And destroy me in the courts? Have you any idea of my success rate? I'd rip you to shreds."

Tom moved closer to the edge, staring out over the mountains as he tried to clear his mind of its angry fog. None of it mattered any more. He'd never speak of it again. Sophie mattered, only Sophie.

"So, you'll tell them all." George's voice sounded breathless.

"I don't think so, George. Let's just drop the whole sorry business," Tom answered, keeping his face turned away, hardly noticing the rain that fell hard now and plastered his hair to his face.

The blow to the middle of his back merely surprised him. Fear only clenched his gut when his feet slid open and his flailing arms couldn't restore his balance on the muddy, crumbling cliff edge. The river, such a long way down, seemed to whirl up to greet him. He knew no hope now, but fear dimmed—pain would be momentary and death the cure. Freedom, come early.

"Sophie!" was all he said.

6
Sophie

I kept in touch with Julian throughout the decades that followed, writing often, and visiting from time to time. Tom and I were lovers for a few years before he met Daphne and got married. She was a good ten years younger than him and socially ambitious. He enjoyed his lifestyle to some extent, but I think he found it oppressive, too. He'd asked me to marry him, but I wasn't ready; and, of course, not only was I barren, but I was still married for all I knew. I never told any of them these things.

About five years into the marriage, we met by chance at the Tate and soon after started to enjoy trysts in nice hotels every month or so, mostly in London. We came together with the same passion as before; those weekends were grand landmarks in my life and in his, I believe. I refreshed him, as he used to put it, and I think I provided him with a solace he never found at home.

Although content with my life for the most part—predictability came as a relief after the mayhem of war—I enjoyed the occasional break from my dreary school and a sojourn in a luxury hotel with meals on a very different plane from my usual fare. Tom sometimes took me shopping for nicer clothing than I could afford on my meager salary. He enjoyed my delight in a pretty dress or blouse. He was a gentle kind man. I'd always liked his looks, too. He had reddish hair and a fair skin and those eyes—I've never seen eyes such a brilliant

green color. He still looked wonderful when I saw him last—
was it only a few days ago?—because his white hair made his
eyes look even more intense. And the sweet smile made me
melt again, just as it used to. While he had a sedentary career,
he told us he played football on the weekends. No wonder his
body looked firm and muscular. Not much taller than me, Tom
was always so quiet and unassuming that people didn't notice
his good looks. I don't think anyone ever knew his body like I
did. I would have quickly pulled him into my bed again under
different circumstances.

I never considered marriage, except for a brief flash
of hope with Tom. Devoting myself to the education of my
charges without asking much of life outside the school seemed a
necessary suppression while I tried to heal my tattered soul.

I'd saved most of my army pay, a little of my teaching
salary, and a small insurance payment from my parents' estate;
my years of teaching gave me a small pension. When I was fifty,
I retired and bought myself a little house in Montpellier, where
the prices were lower than in England and the weather and food
a good deal better. Some of my old students were still around
and remembered me, so it was all very pleasant.

I didn't think Claude would recognize me after so many
years, but nevertheless I made circuitous inquiries. He had been
killed late in the war, shot whilst defending his precious flock
of sheep from a retreating horde of hungry Nazis. I laughed
when I heard it. He'd died as he lived. I retained a notary, dusted
off a pile of old documents, and established my claim to the
abandoned farm—we had never divorced. Soon after, I sold it
to an English couple who wanted to retire to that area. It was a
windfall I had surely earned, and I hope my mother-in-law and
her son are turning in their graves to this day.

Tom came to stay whenever he could get away, and we
enjoyed many afternoons lying on my bed with the warm thyme-
scented Mediterranean breeze wafting across us while we made
love. We would talk about the old days. I began to anticipate

his visits with impatience; I loved him. I wish I'd married him when I had the chance. You don't need children to be happy, do you? But people think you do, that's the problem. Men like to procreate, assure their immortality.

Julian came over a few times, but we didn't sleep together, although I think he hoped we would. He brought Janet once. She didn't seem to like France much, so I was surprised to hear they had bought the inn. I'd sent them up there for a couple of days. I told them how beautiful it was and that the owner was going to retire soon, so they'd better see it while I could get them a discount. He told me later that he'd fallen in love with it on the spot. He spoke French well, so made the owner an offer and sealed it all within a few weeks. He said Janet was too shocked to say much.

I suppose it wasn't fair, he'd given her no choice. But of course she had a choice, we all did. What we lack is courage. I could have left Claude sooner and perhaps saved my baby. Tom could have come to me, no matter what, and been with me still. Janet could have stayed in England and made a new life for herself. George could have kept his mouth shut and found a backbone.

There's nothing heroic about trudging a straight line through life's mire and muck like a tortoise with his eye on a tasty dandelion. It's being willing to make the hard break and face the consequences that tests your mettle. The high road is full of cowards.

7
Daphne

Tom died five days ago and George, I hear, the day after. Just writing that down gives me a jolt. I am a widow. Ugh, that sounds ugly.

I can see the mountains out of the casement window, hard and hateful. They loom over me like fairytale ogres. How am I supposed to carry on without a husband? I didn't take the pills this morning. I'm sick of pills, of being half asleep and half awake, relieved not to think, but at the same time bored, fuzzy-headed, not quite crying, not quite steady. I've got to pull myself together and get on with things; that is what is expected of people like us. No fuss, no scenes.

I've always kept a journal. It helps keep everything straight, especially when I'm in muddle about things, like now. It's very private, even Tom never knew about it. It hasn't always been easy to keep up the social front, because I didn't grow up with all that, and the journal helps. I keep lists, in it, too. What I wore, what the others wore, who said what and how they said it. But I wouldn't like anyone else to read about my worries. Too, too embarrassing. I do it as if I'm writing a letter to a dear sister. Not that I've seen my sister in years. She didn't marry well so she wouldn't have fit in with our friends. No class whatsoever.

Of course, I didn't bring my journal here with me, so I'll have to copy this out when I get home. Or burn the whole damn thing, more likely. I'm sure I won't die for years and years, but I wouldn't want anyone to find it and know how much I've had to struggle to keep up with everything. And everybody. People are always watching, always hoping you'll slip up.

It's never the same when you're not part of a couple any more, I've seen it happen. You're not invited anywhere important and other women don't trust you, especially if you're good-looking like me. It's the husband's position in society that's important, that's the truth of it. The woman tags along, saying and doing the right things, preserving the right appearances. It's a partnership. No partner, no team, and you're through. People can't be bothered with you any more. I've dropped women from our circle when they no longer fit in. That's how it is. There are no real friends after you grow up, just social contacts and contracts. You have to keep up appearances, no matter what. Maybe I'll be able to find another husband; if there's anyone suitable who is available. After a decent interval, naturally.

Sophie gave me some sleeping pills, so I slept off the worst of the shock. I stayed on for a few extra days until I could face the journey. I had to wait for Tom, anyway, I could hardly have left him behind. We got a call through to Ellen on Wednesday, and she'll have told her brother and arranged the funeral. The authorities released Tom's body this morning, so we can fly home tomorrow. Julian said he'd spoken to Ellen himself while I was taking a nap, and that the funeral people would have someone waiting at Heathrow. So glad I don't have to deal with all that unpleasantness.

I wonder what I should wear for the funeral? I'd better take a quick look around Oxford to buy the right sort of dress. A suit, perhaps. Sweet but respectable. Black ages me so; navy with white accents, perhaps.

Ellen said all the right things when I told her the news. She didn't break down, so I can't tell how she feels about losing her father. It doesn't make any difference really, we'll all just have to get on with it. Make do with less, I suppose. I'll have to give up my social life for a few months or people will talk.

I must look into my financial position, too. Tom was a sensible man, so I'm sure he left me well provided for.

That Sophie, I wonder what her story is. When we arrived at this dreadful place, Tom was surprised to see her. Pleased to see her. He said he'd known her during the war and that she'd been a nurse in the hospital he was in. He kept looking at her in a funny sort of a way. I don't believe she's our sort. Not entirely respectable. I heard her talking French very fast to the kitchen staff. Not reliable, I shouldn't think, seems to have gone native. Can't imagine what Julian is doing with a woman like that, although from a man's point of view I suppose anything's better than nothing. She's his bit of fluff. I have a funny feeling she might have been Tom's bit of fluff once. Long ago, of course, long before he met me.

Tom was successful and made a pretty decent living, but he never told me what would happen to the firm if he should die. I was his father's secretary for a while, that's how I met him, so I know a little about how the firm works. Tom became senior partner after his father retired, but there are four or five others now. Barristers can be tricky.

Tom was in all sorts of local organizations and people respected him—and me too, of course. We had a thriving social life, lots of cocktail parties and formal dinners. Our two children both did well at school, although James refused to follow his father, silly boy. Only one more year at the Royal Academy of Music, although goodness knows where that will get him. Certainly not the sort of position in society enjoyed by his father and me. Musicians can be a raffish lot. I was simply furious when Tom backed him up on his choice of study. Ellen went to teacher's training college. Better, although I'll have to see to it that she meets suitable young men—teachers won't do. Julian inherited his social position and the money that went with it, but that's not how it usually is with teachers. They tend to be a drippy lot. Lower middle class, except in the top public schools like Julian's, otherwise they'd have gone into the professions.

I hope no looks down on James if he decides to teach music. He's probably not good enough to earn a living as a performer. I don't know a lot about music, especially his kind. String quartets are very boring, on the whole. I go to some of his concerts because I'm a good mother, and I'm careful to keep a pleasant, interested look on my face. It amazes me that most of the audience seems to enjoy it, but I suspect many of them are playacting, putting on airs because they want people to think they are cultured. But I don't see why people would actually pay good money to go and listen to that sort of thing unless someone they know is playing. Not to mention giving up a Saturday evening. Ridiculous business.

I hope I'll be able to afford to keep up our lovely house. Being just outside Oxford is very convenient. Quiet, but close enough in. I find it a very appropriate house, I must say. That clever old man I found makes our garden the envy of our avenue, at least since our dog died last year—thank God, he kept digging up the herbaceous borders. Mucky things, dogs are, but Tom and the children always insisted on having one. No consideration. And the stupid creature never listened to me, almost as if he knew I didn't like him.

This invitation from Julian came out of the blue. I wasn't really interested because it didn't sound very amusing. And I was right, it hasn't been. There are only four households in this hamlet, cold winds blow over the mountains, it's rained every day, and there's absolutely nothing to do, unless you like to wear sensible shoes and tramp up and down rocky hills all day. Horrid place. When people talk about the South of France, this definitely isn't what they mean.

I did go for a walk with Pamela once. One should always try to keep up with such people. She comes from a very good family and so did George. She slipped a note under my door while I was sedated. It was in one of those very high-class envelopes that have people's titles, names, and addresses embossed on them. George was actually a viscount! Their address is Wandford Hall,

Upper Wandford, Hampshire. No street numbers or anything. I wonder if she'll find widowhood inconvenient? Probably not, not with her background. She's got an estate, for God's sake. And I'm quite sure she's worn the trousers in that family for years. She might have a lover, for all any of us know. I doubt George was much use in that department. Tom used to be, in the early days, but he'd go through periods when he seemed to lose interest, and then pick up again. I didn't really care much. He was pretty lively the night we arrived here. I didn't feel like it (I never do), but he was oddly insistent. He's never pushed himself on me before. Men really are peculiar. You never know what's going through their minds.

I'd almost forgotten, he asked me for a divorce once. Said there was someone else. I refused, of course. What a nerve after all those years and two children! He never pressed it, so she can't have been more than a passing whim. Men go through these phases in middle age, or so one hears. I wonder who she was? Some empty-headed little typist, no doubt. I'm sure I did him a favor.

Disaster hit after we'd been here about three days. We'd gathered on the patio for aperitifs before dinner. It was absolutely freezing and I shivered miserably, even though I'd bundled up. Rain threatened. Again. There was a sort of awkward silence. George was a war hero, badly wounded in France, so I could understand why he didn't always feel like talking. Julian always seemed to have a smirk on his face and puffed on that filthy pipe while he watched everyone. I don't like him much. He's a bit of a know-it-all, fancies himself an intellectual. Well, I suppose he must be an intellectual, but he needn't put on such airs. Pamela, George's wife, is the right sort, but she doesn't dress very well. Doesn't have to in her position. She's got almost black hair that could look absolutely stunning with her fair skin, but it's usually all rats' tails. You are always aware she's around. She has that kind of presence. She didn't seem much interested in the rest of us, but there you are, people in her set do as they like. Sophie chatters much too much, always so frightfully cheerful, but even she seemed to have run out of steam that afternoon. I always try to be sociable and keep the conversation going.

"Tell us about the war, when you all met one another," I said. "Tom never talks about it. Does George talk to you about the war, Pamela?"

"Oh, yes. Frequently." She sounded very off-hand.

"Well," Julian said, "we all met Sophie when she nursed us after we were wounded in Italy. But I was wounded some distance away from Tom and George—we kept getting separated during a chaotic retreat. Remind me of your story, Tom. You and George were wounded together, weren't you?"

"Yes, sort of. And it's quite a story I could tell." Tom paused as if thinking where to begin.

"I'm sick of talking about the war," George shouted, I mean really shouted. Shocking. "Julian, take me for a walk, why don't you. I've hardly been away from the inn at all since I came."

"I offered to take you out, George, but you never wanted to go," Pamela said, sounding terribly annoyed and snappish.

"I'd be glad to take you out tomorrow, George, but I must oversee dinner tonight, I'm afraid," said Julian.

"I'll take you for a spin right now, George. Help you work up an appetite," Tom said as he grasped the handles of the wheelchair and spun it around, rather aggressively, in my opinion. His voice had a hard edge to it, too, a surprising harshness.

"Well, what was all that about?" I asked as they moved up the path. I looked around at each of them, but they dropped their eyes. No one answered except Pamela.

"Absolutely no idea," she said.

That's the last time I saw poor old Tom. They weren't back in time for dinner. The wind had come up and a cold drizzle had been falling for some time by then. Julian said they'd probably taken shelter—although I don't know where they'd find any shelter in this God-forsaken place—and if they didn't show up in an hour, he'd go and look for them. He'd just gone out to his car when George wheeled up the drive dripping wet and sobbing. I just knew something awful had happened.

After George told his story, I felt as though the world had crumbled; my world, I mean. Sophie gave me a couple of sleeping pills and helped me to bed. Some doctor appeared next morning and sedated me right after they told me they'd found Tom, so I missed the death scene, thank God. It seems Pamela didn't come out of this much better, although I didn't know that until yesterday. Apparently, she stayed in her room, said she didn't want to see anyone, and took George back to England this morning. I don't suppose our paths will cross again, more's the pity. Perhaps I'll drop her a note in a couple of months. I know I never want to see Julian and Sophie again, though I have to admit they've been quite kind. I suppose they feel responsible. But we simply have nothing in common. Pamela's more my type. I don't know if she thinks I am her type, though. It's hard to tell with those people.

He didn't deserve to fall off a cliff. He must have been terrified on the way down. Poor old Tom. He really was quite sweet. Dull, but sweet.

8
Sophie

The dream came again last night. I am climbing a mountain of severed limbs that still ooze and drip. I reach the top and stand, bloodied, to look down over a charred and empty landscape. A tank appears on the horizon and I watch it approach, a slow and unstoppable threat as it rolls straight toward me. It stops at the base of the mountain, the barrels tilt up, and I know I'm the target. I expect to die, but instead wake up in a sweating panic.

All I want is a pleasant easy life. No nightmares, no deep passions, I only want to coast along in peace. I once held my parents in contempt for living that way. My father fought in the Great War and never spoke of it. He embraced a meager life, seeking nothing beyond. Was that how he slew his dragons?

Those poor boys were so badly off, so ripped apart. It wasn't just pain I saw in their eyes, there was a pleading there, too, a pleading for reassurance and tenderness, especially from those who were horribly disfigured. The first one I comforted had just had his bandages off. He was perhaps nice looking once, but his face was now a hideous snarl of burned tissue. He retreated from us all, wouldn't look at anyone, even his C.O. One day, when I was giving him his sponge bath, I felt him harden. He looked at me then. I knew what I should do. My body was lost to motherhood, so why not use it for comfort? Love was unthinkable, but affection and compassion still possible. He was the first of many souls I helped bring back. Our chaplain used to think it was all due to his ministrations!

Julian, Tom, and George, all fit and attractive, Tom most of all. Since they were in the same regiment, I used to wonder why Tom and Julian never visited George, although I did once see Tom and George talking in angry hissing whispers. I only heard the story years later.

George was a whiner, even then, although I have to allow he had plenty to complain about. He had his moments, though. His hip was a mess, so I pleased him in ways I wouldn't have in the normal course of things. Whatever constituted normal in those days. He always showed me great tenderness afterwards. I would lie down by his side and caress him wherever it didn't hurt. Eyes half closed, he would stroke my face and whisper endearments that allowed me to forget my own reality. His room lay down an out-of-the-way corridor, so I went to him often, taking care the others didn't notice. I wonder if he ever caressed Pamela that way? I shouldn't think so, she doesn't strike me as the sort of woman a man caresses. He wept the night before the ambulance took him away to a specialist hospital and the agony of more operations. I cried a little, too.

Julian knows Tom and I were lovers at one time, but he doesn't know it went on for thirty years. I only broke it off with Tom when Julian and I got together. I still cared for him, still held him in a niche in my heart, but I needed more. Julian once looked the classical tall, dark, and handsome officer type, striking for his military posture. He's still tall and handsome in a flinty sort of way, although no longer dark-haired. And he is still robust. I like that, need that.

I can't let Julian see the extent of my grief. I don't want to hurt his feelings as he has been very good to me. He's courteous, although rather clumsy in bed, not like poor dear Tom. Tom's mind went a lot deeper, too, he just didn't talk a lot. Julian is cultured, but in many respects superficial in outlook.

Yes, Julian treats me well, but I know he can be callous, the way his kind are conditioned to be. They absorb their assumptions through osmosis, almost from the cradle.

9
Pamela

The hearse took George down to Montpellier on Wednesday. Certain procedures must be performed before he can be transported back to England—an autopsy for one thing, as he hadn't been in the care of a doctor here. Regulations. Julian saw to it all. He'll drive me down to the airport tomorrow.

Just three days since I became a widow, what I've dreamed of for a long time. A wicked thought, I suppose. I feel rather sorry for George now, although I hated him sometimes. Despised is a better word, probably. His whining presence spawned a knot of irritation in me I could never quite get rid of. I had no patience with him, despite his protestations of heroism. He didn't live his life like a hero, gave up on any meaningful existence very quickly, behaved like a weakling, couldn't stick to anything, never even took an interest in his children. I feel very calm now, no knot, just a bit empty. When I rang up the children they were shocked, sounded a bit shaky to me, though they couldn't seem to stand him when he was alive. The blood tie, I suppose. Perhaps they feel sad for what might have been, should have been, what they'd missed.

I still can't quite believe everything happened like it did. I hope to God no one breathes a word to Daphne. We've only been here six days and our lives have changed immeasurably. I suppose I'll go on much as before, but poor Daphne is one of those ambitious women forever jockeying for her ideal of position and possession. If all her friends are like that, she'll have a rough go of it. I'll be perfectly happy, but I think she'll be miserable until she finds a new husband to prop her up.

I was quite intrigued when we got Julian's letter. It's a change for me to be free of the estate. I love the work, but it does take a lot out of one. My son will manage very well until I get back—in fact, perhaps it's time to think about turning everything over to him. George seemed ambivalent about the trip. I must say I pushed it rather. Poor old Tom, he didn't deserve that. George did, though.

We thought we were to be the only guests. It clearly came as a shock to George to see them all here. I observed him closely, how he watched everyone, how nervous he seemed. There were undercurrents I couldn't quite fathom, though I understand it all now.

I unpacked our things and we all gathered in the lounge to find Julian had set drinks and hors d'oeuvres outside.

"I thought we'd have drinks on the patio," Julian said, "the weather is a little cool, but still pleasant. The cook is preparing a simple supper. We'll have a special dinner tomorrow night when you have all recovered from your trip."

He led us out onto a patio where we had a lovely view of the Cevennes—plateaux rather than mountains. Wildflowers grew in profusion up the slope to the right side of the patio, and a swimming pool ahead of us mirrored the last rays of the sun. Romantic in the right company. Gorgeous. I was thinking how I might make a little haven like this on the estate, on the south side of the manor, perhaps, but I've gone off the idea. We sipped our drinks in silence for a few minutes.

"The pool is heated," Julian told us, "so you'll find it quite pleasant."

"Did you have a great deal of renovation to tackle when you bought the place?" Tom asked. "I imagine all this old stonework takes some keeping up."

"No, it was a going concern when we bought it, and everything was in good condition. We moved in on a Friday, and had our first guests on the Saturday. We were frantic trying to learn the ropes. We didn't even know how to handle traveler's checks or credit cards! Thank God for good help. We have a marvelous cook, as you'll soon find out." Julian has an irritating habit of making an almighty palaver of emptying, filling, and lighting his pipe. We all watched him go at it with a strange sort of bored fascination.

Daphne broke the spell with her shrill voice, "Don't you mind having strange people in your own home all the time? I should absolutely hate being at everyone's beck and call." She wasn't born to that accent, there's too much push behind it.

"Oh no, I don't mind. My late wife Janet often felt overwhelmed, but then she was ill, although we didn't know it at the time," said Julian.

George, I think wanting to feel part of the group, said, "I suppose you meet some interesting people." He gripped the wheelchair armrests as if he might be afraid of taking flight, and his color seemed high compared with his usual pallor.

"Yes, I do. When you chat with them after dinner, you find out all sorts of things about them that they would probably never divulge to family or friends. Of course, the liqueurs help, and the feeling of being adrift from their everyday lives. People are more interesting than they know."

"Yes, and I find that people are rarely what they seem. Don't you agree, George?" Tom said.

"Oh, I don't know about that. I don't see many people," George muttered. His color rose alarmingly towards purple. There was something between those two. Of course, Tom hadn't expected to find George here any more than George had expected to see him.

"Well, let's go in to eat," Julian said, seeming amused.

The food was excellent and the conversation quite good, although George contributed little beyond his usual peevish comments. Only Julian and Sophie talked to him, at first. I knew he wouldn't be able to resist alluding to his medal—although I didn't know it then, asking for trouble under the circumstances, but he never did have any common sense. I noticed it got Daphne to prick up her ears, though, and she simpered at him once or twice in the most revolting manner. Sophie was charming but, somehow, inscrutable. I can't quite place her. She seems more French than English in some ways, but is, I suspect, passionless under the charm. She's suffered. George drank too much wine as usual and retired early.

Oh lord, Julian's come again. He is being very kind, but I do wish he wouldn't hover. Feels responsible, I suppose. I'd like to be left alone with my thoughts for a while.

"Oh, hello Julian."

"I don't want to intrude, Pamela, but I thought you could do with a brandy. Bit of a shock, eh?"

"How kind. Yes, perhaps it would help. It's all been a bit of a blow. I think I always knew in my heart that George wasn't the stuff of heroes, but there was the medal, wasn't there?"

"Yes, there was the medal, Pamela. Tom did contest it, through channels, but it didn't get him anywhere, in fact, it went against him. The brass thought it bad form. I warned him our C. O. had fought in the Great War with George's father, but he wouldn't let it go. He should have had the medal, you know. What did he tell you about that day we were wounded?"

"George told me his story, many times, and anyone else who'd listen. He said you found yourselves cut off from your unit as you retreated after a terrible battle. A few Germans pursued you, so George hid in a henhouse to get a better shot at them. The Germans heard the chickens clucking. A couple burst in and George shot them and came out shooting. Thinking he'd got them all, he made for the back of the farmhouse where he'd last seen Tom. He'd almost reached Tom when a grenade hit the house, wounding them both. George got the last German in the chest. I didn't doubt that part of the story, he's always been an excellent shot. Anyway, they dragged their way back and found you. The three of you somehow found your comrades, a heroic effort on his part with such dreadful wounds. You were all treated in a field hospital and evacuated to England. See, I know it by heart! Pathetic."

I feel unaccountably sad after reciting that tale. It's the last time. I do wish Julian would go away.

"Yes, pathetic it is. He was always a spoiled brat, but I'd never have taken him for a coward. But you know, Pamela, sometimes soldiers lose their nerve and do something they're ashamed of, but they soon get back in the saddle. We don't really know that George wouldn't have come through, do we?"

"I hadn't thought of it that way. You could be right, but then I think he would have kept quiet about it all, not boasted about his exploits at every opportunity. No, he was a coward."

"Did he run the estate well?"

"No, I've always managed it, at least since his father died in 1941. Once he was feeling better, I think he felt the need to assert control over his affairs, but he didn't have the self-discipline to stick to it and he soon lost interest. He seemed relieved when I took back the reins.

"He didn't know what to do with himself, and he told us time and again he deserved more attention when he complained about his health, but I hadn't any patience with his whining. He said his life was hell, and a hero deserved more, but he lacked the backbone to change anything. Believe it or not, he complained that the children were a nuisance, although he had seemed to welcome their arrival—probably as affirmation of his manhood. He insisted on sending them off to boarding school as soon as they had finished kindergarten."

"They must have resented that."

"Well, it's not uncommon in our set, is it? But, I have to say they kept their distance. Anyway, after a few years, he claimed he couldn't walk, but as I said, I sometimes looked through his study window and saw him pacing up and down, picking up this book and that, utterly aimless."

"Pamela, I'm so, so sorry. I hope you'll find some peace now. And George, too."

"Thank you Julian. Do you mind if I spend some time alone?"

"Of course, not. See you in the morning. We should leave by nine. Sleep well."

I hope I sleep soundly, that my last memory of George won't haunt my dreams. He looked like a terrified rabbit cornered by dogs. I hadn't looked him full in the face for years, and saw with stunning clarity how diminished he was. I'm sure my disgust showed on my face, must have been the last thing he saw. He dropped his glass when Julian accused him of killing Tom. While the stroke overcame him, the smell of the spilled scotch tickled my nostrils, and I wondered why no one cleaned it up. Funny thing to be thinking when your husband is dying right in front of you.

I stopped Sophie when she moved to help him. It was best to let him go, let the story die with him. I asked for their silence. The children must never know, his cowardice would devastate them. And there's no need for Daphne to know my husband killed hers, either.

I need to get home. My neighbor has been my friend and lover for a long time now. His wife died about ten years ago. We never meet at either house. Staff always gossip too much, it's about the only excitement they can expect in their walk of life. We refurbished his old gamekeeper's cottage together, and it's a delightful hideaway. I need him now, need his strength and passion. Who knows, maybe he'll propose— after a decent interval, of course. He's no viscount, some would call him nouveau riche, but who gives a damn? Of course, he may not propose, and it's always possible he'll be scared off by my availability. We'll see. I don't want to lose him, but I'll not grovel.

I never expected to find myself in love at my time of life.

10
Sophie

I was curious about this reunion, too, so I can't really blame Julian, although he didn't handle it very well. He doesn't understand deep emotion, it's just not in him. He had no idea what he might set loose. I should have realized, but I didn't. Maybe I've become like him, a surface thinker. I've been a surface feeler for years. I should have remonstrated with him when he made his amusement so obvious.

Dear old Tom, so many years since I tried to get him away from that dreadful Daphne, but it was too late for us. She threatened to ruin him. I fantasized about him last night, remembered his touch. How I hunger for his touch.

And Pamela, what will she do now? Look for someone she can love? I don't think she's loved or been loved for years. Her demeanor is too flat.

I've never felt passion for Julian, just affection and an easygoing intimacy. I caught him staring at me yesterday. He had a hangdog look, as if he were mooning after me. Does he suspect the depth of my grief? Is he afraid of losing me? Is he capable of deep feeling? Perhaps I should ask him, but I don't know what I'd do with the answer. I don't know if I can stand his touch again. He started a rockslide that killed two people. I'm no better, I should have recognized the danger, and I should have put a stop to it.

Such a terrible, cruel scene. When George got back to the inn that night, wet and cold, and cried out, "I think Tom's dead," I was too shocked to react for the moment. Daphne screamed and hunched herself into a chair. Julian paled and started to shake.

"What happened, George?" Pamela asked.

"He stopped my chair under a tree while he went to look at the river from the cliff top. I struggled up to relieve myself, and when I sat back down I couldn't see him any more. It was very upsetting for me, to feel alone in a strange place." George coughed and gagged slightly; he seemed short of breath. "It started to rain, and I went looking for him, going as close to the edge as I dared, but he was nowhere to be found. I don't know what happened, he must've slipped in the mud. I couldn't help it, I did my best. You'd better call the police. I'm so cold and tired. It's all so terribly upsetting." No one spoke, not even Daphne, and no one moved to comfort him. Even under the circumstances, his self pity served as an irritant.

I took Daphne to her room and gave her a couple of sleeping pills I found in the medicine cabinet. I sat with her until she slept, assuring her that the police would start searching immediately, although I knew they couldn't do much until daybreak. I went back to the sitting room and sank into a sofa. Pamela had taken George off to bed by then. I wondered if a weakling in a wheelchair could have killed a fit man. I knew that George was under the impression that no one else knew the real story of his cowardice. He could have felt Tom might have been tempted to talk now we were all together again.

Julian came in and told me he had called the police and asked them to search for Tom. He still trembled. I looked into his drawn face, but he couldn't meet my eyes. What had we unleashed with this foolish reunion? Had George managed to silence Tom?

They found Tom early next morning. He hadn't fallen that far, just to a wide ledge about three meters below the overhang, but it seems he'd knocked his head on a rock and broken his neck. Apparently there was a strange circular welt on his back as if he had bounced off the end of a tree branch, although there wasn't a tree nearby. A gendarme arrived after lunch and questioned George, who expressed horror and the helplessness of one confined to a wheelchair. We all agreed that Tom had not appeared at all despondent, and the gendarme left satisfied that a terrible accident had occurred. The doctor I called in sedated Daphne after we broke the news. The rest of us gathered in the sitting room. Julian made drinks for everyone and sat down near the fire. A thick silence fell.

George slumped in his robe and slippers as he considered his scotch and sighed like a martyr. I looked him over, appraising him as if he were a wax model of someone I used to know. He had been good looking once, tall with broad shoulders and thick chestnut hair. He had a paunch now, his shoulders stooped, and his legs were purple-veined and stick thin. His hair, too, was diminished and had acquired the stippled shades of fireplace ashes. His face had the downturned cast of incessant petulance. He'd developed a tic in his right cheek overnight, and his eyes wandered, lighting here and there like a fly in a hot room. His breath sounded labored. It was not a good likeness of the George I once knew.

"Well, well," he blurted with a sharp laugh, "so it's all over for old Tom."

Another silence ensued while we absorbed his hateful words.

Julian finally spoke. "What really happened, George? We know you were angry with Tom, and some of us know why."

"What in hell do you mean by that," George screamed, dropping his glass. "Know what? What?"

"We know the story of your cowardice," Julian answered, leaving the glass where it fell. "Tom told me years ago. We know you didn't deserve that medal, that you were just lucky shooting your way out of the hole you had hidden yourself in.

"He told me, too, George," I said. "What happened? Did he threaten to expose you?"

"Lies, lies, all of it! I'm a hero, everyone said so, and I've got the medal to prove it," George said, his voice breaking like an adolescent's.

"Tell me your version, Julian," said Pamela in a strong, cold voice.

"Yes, it's time you knew the truth."

As Julian told the miserable tale, Pamela stood behind the wheelchair facing us as if coiled to spring, her hard blue eyes wide and furious, her clenched fists held to her thighs.

"I always thought there was something fishy about that medal," she said, standing in front of George now. "I knew you didn't have the makings of a hero, you are the coward I thought you might be, and perhaps you're a cold-blooded killer, too. I don't know what to tell your son if this ever gets out. His father is nothing, worse than nothing."

Her hands clenched and unclenched, and for a moment I thought she might punch him.

"I cleaned caked mud off the bottom of your shoes last night. You were walking. I knew you could walk, I've watched you pacing about in your study and then coming out in your wheelchair, whining and looking for pity. You killed him, didn't you? You pushed him over the edge. What did you use? A stick, a tree branch? I heard that gendarme mention the mark on poor Tom's back. What did you do, George?"

As tears rolled down George's puce face, we all leaned forward slightly like old tombstones, stony and mute.

He looked Pamela in the eye as if mesmerized. "He was going to tell, had to stop him," he said, croaking as if racked with pain. With a sudden look of surprise, his eyebrows arched and he gasped loudly, almost greedily. His face cooled to ivory and he panted, reaching out as if trying to claw himself forward. His chest rose and fell with effort, stopped briefly, then started its struggle again. His eyes still locked onto Pamela's.

"Looks like a stroke," I said, moving toward him, but Pamela raised her hand to stop me. I stayed where I was and watched. Just watched.

Pamela continued to look into George's gray face. "I know he killed Tom, but we'll never prove it. Let him go, and let his disgrace die with him. Can I ask for your silence? The children must never know. His cowardice would devastate them. And there's no need for Daphne to know he killed Tom."

Julian murmured his assent, fixated as he was on George's last battle. I just nodded, going against all I had stood for during my nursing career. I'd held nothing back in those days, but George had been found wanting. Love of my fellow man and reverence for life long ago assumed a practical tilt.

The sudden stench signaled it was over. Pamela rushed out, hand clasped to her mouth as if she wanted to vomit. Understandable, she'd never seen the carnage we had.

11
Claude

The cart rounded the bend and his home came into view at last. He'd spent many years in London, but instead of settling down, he'd begun to feel like an exile. He spoke good English, but what difference would that make now? He turned to her with a smile to share his excitement and happiness, but she turned away and frowned as she looked over the old house. She could not share his feelings, could not bring herself to feel happy for his sake. Sophie had been a mistake. He should have married one of his own kind. He looked at her again, so pretty and spoiled. How could he have imagined he could make a life with her? She had turned his head with her adoring ways and her ravenous need. These girls and the fairy tales they dreamed up about weddings! Real marriage can never live up to those dreams.

Edgy now, he wondered how the first meeting would go. His mother could be difficult. She had had a hard life, and so she, in turn, had become hard; perhaps she had always been so. And she did not trust foreigners, or people who came from cities. She was right.

Sophie should appreciate that his home was a real home. Nothing fancy, none of the little gadgets and pretty furniture he'd seen in her house. But people had lived in his house for hundreds of years, people who had birthed and died, loved and fought. Those walls absorbed their sounds and feelings, held them in forever.

They had hardly spoken on the long journey. She changed after he'd come home drunk one night and flung himself on her and used her without "protection" as she liked to call it. She was no longer a virgin, but a married woman; it was his right, and it had soon been over anyway. His father had often been drunk, and he had heard what he did with Maman, just as he had listened to the noisy births of his brothers and sisters. His mother had grunted most of the way through, but would let out a roar or two towards the end as she pushed the baby out, much like any animal would, but that was about all. She soon got out of bed and back to work. She never complained. She was strong, bred from strong stock.

He had written her a letter, which Father Bertrand should have read to her by now, so he hoped she expected them, had had enough time to prepare herself. Maman would not like Sophie. What had he been thinking? He was married now, though, stuck with it.

A large box lay outside the front door. His black-clad mother stepped over the threshold when she heard the cart, and his heart fidgeted as his mouth hung open. Her clasped hands posed between her breasts where they touched her waist. Never a good sign. Her mouth, tight and rolled in, failed to stretch into a smile of welcome.

He got down and helped Sophie out of the cart, not easy in her condition. She had not grown that big yet, but she was not used to carts. Stupid girl, it could not be that different from getting on and off a London bus. He wanted to embrace his mother, but she looked hard and unwilling. He watched the two women stare at each other. Sophie moved towards Maman with her hand outstretched, but the old woman took a step back and clicked her feet together.

"Etienne," his mother called out to the cart owner. "You will take me to my sister's house!"

"Oui Madame." A surly reply, and it would be all over the village by nightfall.

"Claude, you are a foolish boy. Did you expect me to share my house, my kitchen with this foreign woman?"
She clambered up into the cart unassisted and gestured to Etienne to load her box; no one spoke. Claude and Sophie watched until she disappeared out of sight around the same bend they had come from not ten minutes before.

"Come in," was all he could muster.

He saw how Sophie wrinkled her nose. The smell of the house was dear and familiar to him, but she was accustomed to lavender-scented polish. She pointed at the range and asked what it was. She had no idea! When he told her that they cooked using wood as fuel, she gasped, picked up one of her cases and took it upstairs. He could hear her walking around. She came downstairs slowly, using a hand on the wall to steady herself. He recalled the wooden stair rails in her house. No space for them in that narrow opening. She'd get used to it.

"Claude, I couldn't find the bathroom. There is a bathroom, isn't there?"

"Yes, it is outside. There, see?" He moved to the window and pointed out the fine stone outhouse. "It must be emptied every week or so, but do not worry, I will do it for you. My mother has always done it, but I know you are not used to such things."

She went out and soon returned. Her face had become like that of the stone Madonna in the village church. White, cold, lifeless. She wandered around for a few minutes, peering into corners and out of each window.

"Claude, I am not like your mother." Said without heat, but it hit him hard. She despised them, she despised his home.

"No, you are not anything like my mother." He made his voice equally toneless.

He opened the corner cupboard. Maman had left them some food, good of her under the circumstances. A piece of lamb, some carrots and potatoes, bread and cheese. He got them out and laid them on the table. He checked the range. Plenty of kindling.

"As you are new at this, you had better start preparing dinner now. It will take some time since you are not used to it. Here, I will start the fire. The pans are on that shelf by the side of the window."

"I have no idea how to cook on that stove. Why don't you cook and I'll watch."

She actually expected her husband to cook! She was unwilling even to try.

"I expect my wife to be good for something. I expect you to cook the food, clean this house, wash the clothes, and help outside when I need you to. You must grow up, Sophie, this is your home now. You are a housewife, and soon to be a mother."

"Well, it's not much of a home, is it? You've seen where I come from. How could you have brought me to such a place? You know I've never lived in a hovel, so how do you expect me to know how to manage one?"

He hit her then, reddening her cheek. She ran upstairs and he did not see her again that night. He opened a bottle of strong local wine and drank it all. Then he stumbled up the stairs and slept alone, as he would for the rest of the marriage. She told him to stay out of her bed for the duration of her pregnancy in case he harmed the baby. He was so rough in love, she threw at him. She had liked that once, but she did not like anything about him now. He stayed away from her bed, more out of pride than anything.

She began to manage the house, not like Maman, but she took care of the basics. She cooked barbaric food like all the English, so he walked over to his aunt's house to eat dinner when he could. He never took Sophie. Her face always showed what she felt and so did Maman's.

When the pains started he wondered if having a new baby to take care of might make a difference, might soften her feelings for him. He should have gone for the doctor, but his best ewe was giving birth to twin lambs and seemed to be in difficulty. He could not afford to lose her. There was a bad storm brewing, too, and it was not as if he could ask for his mother's help. He knew for a fact that his mother had given birth twice alone, so there could not be that much to it. Pedigree ewes were different. They could be delicate.

By the time he got back upstairs, cold, wet and tired, it was over. All she'd managed to produce was a bloody mess on the sheets and a blue lifeless creature that should have been his son at the foot of the bed. Sophie, pale and weak, demanded a doctor. He went out again, tired as he was, because he knew if he did not and something bad happened to her, he would be blamed.

He felt sad and tired all the time after that. As he watched the tiny coffin go down into the same earth that nurtured his sheep, he thought he understood something of the mystery, the arc of life; but that understanding brought no comfort, only a sense of helplessness.

Sophie left him at the gravesite. Simply walked away and took a taxi back to her other life. The doctor reassured him that mothers took these things hard. She needed a little respite, that was all. She would be back. But she never returned and never wrote. She discarded him like a dirty sock.

Maman came back to take care of him and life fell into a satisfactory rhythm. He sometimes went into town and visited the little brothel behind the church, and that was all he needed. He had his farm, his home, the life he knew. He did not feel comfortable with any of the local girls he met. They seemed so hard. They behaved too much like Maman, which was fine for a Maman, but trouble in a wife in his opinion. He remembered how she used to berate Papa from morning till night when he was sober. When Papa sought solace in wine, he repaid her in the bedroom with violent assaults, and she took it, rather than suffer a beating in front of her children. Of course, with five children in a small house, they heard everything. When he grew old enough to understand such things, he realized that most or all of them had probably been conceived in violence rather than love. Well, what difference did it make? Olivier had been conceived in love, drunk or not, and his bitch of a mother let him die.

His sister had married young and his brothers left for jobs elsewhere. They could not wait to get away, and he had lost touch with all of them. He loved his home, his farm, and had always been Maman's favorite, so she threw herself into his care. He had broken her heart when he left for London. He must follow his star, he'd explained. But it had been a false star, too bright, and he had been glad to get back where he belonged.

One night, after enjoying a particularly entertaining visit to Madame Dumain with one of his friends—they had shared a delightfully nimble young lady—they dropped in on the bar next door. They drank too much, sang too much, and talked too much. He'd told a couple of farmers about his wife and about what a mistake it had all been. One of them asked him why he did not get an annulment. He had never heard of such a thing. Marriage is forever, he had always been taught. "Ask Father Bertrand," the man said.

The annulment took a few years and proved expensive. Maman, so strict in her religious practices, and so careful with money, paid for everything. She craved grandchildren. He did not see fit to mention he was not especially keen on settling down quite yet, but he wanted to be free from the idea of being tethered to Sophie in any way.

His annulment freed him when he was thirty-four and Maman died when he was thirty-five, urging him to marry with her last breath. He had fetched the doctor too late for her, too.

He'd thought seriously about finding a wife now he was truly alone. But, war broke out, and he worked himself half to death trying to provide extra meat and milk to feed a starving population. After a few hard years, the fighting seemed to have died down and people said the war might be over in a few months. He took to carrying Papa's old rifle because small bands of deserting Boches hid in the mountains in the hope of avoiding capture by either side, and they raided the farms from time to time. It would be nice to take things easier. Perhaps he would hire a couple of laborers. While many soldiers had died, there must be plenty who would come back looking for work. He had only escaped fighting because he was a farmer, but some of the families around had several sons and they could not afford to support them all. The war had been good to him so he had ample savings now, and his mother had left a substantial wad of notes and coins in the bedroom wall.

He thought of marriage again. He had only just turned forty-one and anyway, some women prefer a mature man. He had been alone far too long.

Claude had no illusions about romance. He would pick carefully this time, perhaps a widow with strong sons, boys he could mold into good caretakers of his land and who would take care of him in old age. Or, better, a woman who could give him his own son.

She must be strong, resilient, and know her duty and understand many things without having to be told, and they would be loyal to each other. One of those things she would understand is that a few visits to Madame Dumain had nothing to do with loyalty, had everything to do with a man's wellbeing, a wife's burden eased. The local women knew better than to fuss about these things; they kept their counsel. Passion would turn into comfortable accommodation, and his wishes and comfort would be of paramount importance.

He should ask Father Bertrand, he would know who was who. But she must be from the Languedoc. This was his understanding of marriage: a man and his woman, pulling through life together, rooted in the same soil.

12
Sophie

I am going to visit my son now. Olivier, a name that Claude picked. I couldn't consider naming him at the time. I've never thought of him as Olivier, never thought of him as anything but that little blue floppy body, and he is only an idea now. Or is there more to it? I can't make up my mind about these things. Heaven, Hell, easy metaphors, easy platitudes and comforts, simplistic promises of reward, threats of retribution.

The path is still narrow, still rocky, the cemetery tangled and overgrown. Doesn't anyone tend the dead anymore? But, look, they don't even tend the church. There are so few Catholics left around here since the British started buying all the old properties, it's been closed up. Unprofitable, so the church has abandoned the living, too. I know where to find the grave, the way the path branches off toward it forms a clear map in my mind. Odd, there's a neat border clipped around it. Someone has planted flowers there and cleared the marker free of moss. I stand in front of it, confront the inscription.

"Olivier." I said that aloud for the first time ever. "Olivier." It gets easier.

"Olivier, your mother let a man die this week. I watched him die and didn't help because his wife didn't want me too. We must never speak of it, but I can tell you. I can tell you anything, I think. I suppose it was for the best. But it doesn't feel right. He suffered little, I think, the stroke would have blunted his senses.

Do you know anything, see me, hear me, Olivier? I'm leaving now, going back up the mountain. I'll be back. I won't abandon you again. But for you, I suppose forty years would have passed like a swallow's swoop around a church spire."

I have to get away. From what, to what? I must find peace, but I don't know where to look. I will go back up the mountain to the old stone inn, at least for now. Julian loves me, he has strong arms and a kind, shallow heart. I've made compromises all my life. Why stop now? It's better than nothing, and nothing is empty and frightening.

Those other dreams started again this week, the ones with the starving stick people who live behind glass. I can see them and they can see me. They see I have food, but I can't get through the glass wall, can't stop them lying down to die before my eyes. Can't get through.

I should have made the hard break, taken a different turn at the crossroads, saved my son, and saved myself, too. You see, Olivier, your mother is not a hero.

Who tends the little grave?

Mousetrap

I

This painting draws me in, holds me close. A pensive woman with wispy brown hair like mine sits alone in a garden, serious, but not unhappy, I think. Is she a widow, too? Does she grieve, is she relieved? A woman needed a man then. Mine's gone now, so I can do as I like, at least that's how things are supposed to work these days. I suspect she feels sad and free at the same time. Of course, I'm projecting my own turmoil onto her, but that's what art is for, to wake you up, make you think, fuel your dreams.

They'd never believe where I am and what I'm doing, this mother, this housewife, this nobody. I want to be someone different, someone who sits in the Tate and stares into paintings, who might have an informed opinion about those masterpieces to share with the sort of friends I used to have and want to have again. Bubble, bubble, it's all bubbling up. When I was little I used to hate it when my biggest bubbles burst, popping, losing form, losing sheen, becoming nothing more than a damp blot.

A man has been sitting next to me for at least ten minutes. He sidled in so silently I jumped when he flopped down. He carries a strong whiff of aftershave, sweet and sharp enough to make my jaws ache as if I'd sucked on a lemon. Not many people sit in front of one painting and stare at it like this. Would it be forward to say hello? But it's a new me; the new me speaks up. I sit taller, brace myself to break into the lovely silence.

"Is this the first time you've seen this painting?"

"No, I often come. She reminds me of my wife."

I turn my head slowly because I don't want to startle him like he startled me thudding onto the bench like a sack of turnips. No one likes being startled. He still stares at her, so I stare at him. He's sitting on his hands. It's only September, he can't be that cold. I see nothing unseemly, nothing moving, nothing furtive and nasty. I hate it when people act furtive and nasty. He turns sharply, aggressively. His eyes look strange, always changing slightly; now gray and brown swirled into a soft eddy in an opaque mist, then a harder shade, almost blue.

"Did you lose your wife?"

"In a way. She's a schizophrenic. She used to enjoy that kind of serenity before her mind betrayed us. Now she's been put away I don't see her much. She's gone, to all intents and purposes."

"How dreadful. I am sorry."

We each turn away and again fall silent. What an odd way to put it. Betrayed us. Who talks about people being put away any more? Tom used to threaten to have me put away, and so did Daddy. Men can't stand it when women get emotional, they just can't cope. They try all the control tricks in their repertoire—if this, do that or else, and so on. I never fell for it. Except that dear old Daddy actually did put me in one of those places once, when I was too young to do anything about it. Hold you down, put you away, silence you. That is their way, men.

This man would have been the one to do the putting away. It's so cold the way he's written her off as if she were a lame racehorse. I mustn't judge him too fast; maybe he's simply courageous enough to face the hard reality. People are always judging me, saying I'm odd, imagine things. People are troubled by anyone different enough to ruffle their little lives. Any spark might fan the flames they fear—flames that cast light, show things up. I wonder what he's imagining as he looks at this painting and remembers her.

Mousetrap

I feel a spark in his presence, and his eyes certainly ruffled me. He must have been through a lot, having a crazy wife. My back hurts from leaning forward too tightly, clenching fists and thoughts. Relax, let the muscles soften, pretend someone strokes my back, soothes and adores me.

His voice cuts through my quiet. "What about you, I haven't seen you here before, and I come here nearly every day." His voice sounds flat, robotic and at odds with the overdose of aftershave. Perhaps depression seeks out a jolt of some kind. He needs cheering up. People are always trying to cheer me up and I find it annoying because I dislike an excess of cheerfulness. It masks what's really going on, smears too much crap over the misery that nests inside most of us. Cheerfulness makes people think they needn't pay attention, although a little is acceptable.

"No, I haven't been in the Tate since I was twenty. My family was never interested and they've kept me busy for years. My husband's funeral was yesterday. I've been wondering if she's a widow, if she's sad." What a long speech for Little Mouse, as Tom used to call me if he were in a good mood.

No response. I turn and he's staring at me instead of her. Has he noticed the likeness? He's an unusual man, and yet ordinary in many ways. He's medium everything, even his coloring—not unlike Tom, although his demeanor is very different. But there is something about those eyes, something disturbing. Not disturbing in a bad way. Unsettling is a better word, perhaps, because his eyes lack the usual human veil, are more like a deep well you could drown in. And his odor doesn't fit. It belongs to a shyster like one of Tom's cronies, or, with a lighter touch, to someone more distinguished. Funny how I'm thinking more keenly now. His scented cloud must have pushed off the fog that often clouds my mind.

"You're not very sad, are you? You're escaping from all those well-meaning people mouthing condolences. And your children."

"How do you know that? And how do you know I have children?" I feel uneasy now; surely I'm not that easy to read. "I sat in front of this painting because I want to understand her."

"What you want to understand is yourself. And you look like a mother. Let's go. It's teatime."

He stands suddenly, and, just as suddenly, I find myself on my feet, following him like a hen behind a rooster. An old pattern. Let me hear what this odd stranger has to say, let's see what I make of him before I break free. What does he mean, look like a mother? My tummy is quite flat. It must be my breasts, full breasts that once leaked milk my children were never allowed to taste, that ached for their greedy little mouths, that now ache for a lover's hunger.

We are walking down streets now, turning corners. I'm always turning corners. Not to worry, there are plenty of people around. He strides ahead, leads me away in silence.

I should be at home with my sad children, but I don't feel like it. They can mourn on their own. Soon Stephen will ask for money to tide him over, and his sister will demand a donation for yet another good cause. They want many things. I have no doubt they want me to sell up and live somewhere smaller, by which they mean cheaper. I earned that house, and I mean to stay in it and build my own circle of friends who will visit me there. Not Tom's friends, mine. And I will get rid of that scurvy housekeeper, Mrs. Dutton. Tom installed her, and Old Snotty—solicitors should be smart and slick, not a sad old sack like him—says he has executive power over my affairs and she's to stay. He's always hanging around. Maybe he fancies her, although I can't imagine anyone fancying either of those two. He calls her Nurse Duncan. Apparently, she was a nurse once, but now she's just a housekeeper, so she's quite come down in the world. She always looks as if she's got a toothache. Maybe they act out nurse fantasies. I'd love to catch them at it. It's fun watching people have sex. They always look really stupid and disgusting, but it's exciting all the same.

Tom wasn't always so bad. When he knew his life was nearing its end he became quite tender, almost like the young Tom, but without the compelling ambition that turned him hard and cunning.

"You're not so bad, old girl," he told me last week. "You might find someone who wants you. You're quite a good cook after all." Then he fell asleep. He always fell asleep right after making love, too—making love being a euphemism for what we occasionally did, which was have quick dry sex, nothing more. Tom had left love behind, and love no longer recognized him.

As he weakened, Tom relapsed into the soft northern burr was once part of his charm, the voice he replaced with a hard nasal accent he considered sophisticated. It never quite worked, sounded forced, and sometimes it slipped.

This is a long walk. I should look up and pay attention, but I'm busy.

Did you think people were fooled, Tom, did you really? You weren't a stupid man, you must have known people didn't think much of you. They respected your money, but despised the things you did to get it. I didn't like you much, either, not after the first few years. The first shady deal led you down the easy street that is always perilous — I know all about the councilwoman you fucked to get your first fat contract and I tuned out of your business affairs from then on.

I asked you once if you'd ever fucked another woman since we got married and you had a fit. You didn't mind the question as much as you minded your ladylike wife saying fuck. What a mass of contradictions you were, you with your own foul mouth. Of course, you'd deflected the question nicely.

You lost yourself on the way to the bank, and you got away with it until a few months ago when it became plain you couldn't buy yourself out of an early and difficult death. I used to wonder sometimes if those small dishonesties ever ate into you like the cancer did. Sometimes you had a strange way of lapsing into a sort of trance—what we used to call a brown study—when you looked tired and sad, often fearful. Did guilt and fear lure the cancer into making its bid for a hostile takeover? I'm not sure you ever knew what guilt felt like, though.

Your son admired you and plows his way through life like you. Your daughter took another path, a feeble protest against everything you believed in. She'd have been called a hippie once. You left your mark on them, Tom, but why haven't I? Perhaps because they never saw me as a whole person, only a doormat they wiped their feet on as they came in to dinner.

Good grief, I'm talking to a dead man! I'm going gaga. At least I kept it all in my too busy head.

This bitterness is only going to make me old and shrewish and I must learn to leave it all behind. I let it all happen, never pushed back in the early days. Tom was Tom and I didn't insist on being me, whoever me might have been. No self confidence, no self esteem. There are all kinds of magazine articles now about what low self esteem will do to a girl, but they'd never heard of it in my young days, and wouldn't have paid any attention if they had. I'm only forty-eight, still young enough. Young enough for what, though?

He's standing outside a rundown café, the type that serves big cups too full of dark sweet tea that slops over into the saucer. He waits for me to catch up and opens the door for me. A gentleman, then. He selects a table in the back. The only other customers are an elderly couple without enough teeth between them to make a full set, and a pimply teenaged boy. Did he select this place, or were we just wandering? I should've paid attention.

"Two for tea, tea for two?" The waitress has a jolly lined face and an irritating bantering tone. He raises his eyebrows at me. I nod.

"Two teas, two currant buns." He looks down at his clasped hands. The dry knuckles are white and a tic has started up in his left cheek. I'm glad of his aftershave—it gives a welcome lift to this stale place. He lapses into silence again. I only nod at the waitress when she brings our order because I'm not in the mood for her brand of repartee—as worn and yellowed as her uniform. He still looks down, so I do, too, my mind flooding again.

"I'm having a conservatory and indoor pool put on the side of the house," Tom said one September evening in his harsh "don't argue" tone.

"That's a bit sudden!"

"I've been thinking about it for awhile. Getting a couple of quotes. Be available to let the contractor in on Monday morning, and don't say a word. Don't want him to know anything I don't want him to know. No opinions."

"What could I tell him, Tom? I'm totally in the dark."

"Best that way, dear. Don't bother your pretty little head about it, I'll see to everything." He did, and it was beautiful.

I hate swimming because I got caught in an undertow in Frinton once and nearly drowned. It's painful to draw water into your lungs, terrifying being unable to breathe. An alarming beefy woman on the beach noticed me flailing and hauled me out. "Where is your mother for God's sake?" she bellowed. I suppose she thought ten—and I was a small ten—too young to be on the beach alone. She was right, of course. Between gags and splutters I explained that my mother was ill in the hotel room, which was true enough. She had a hangover, but I left that bit out. Daddy was on a business trip with his secretary, Daphne, which is what set Mummy off again. I didn't mention that, either. The woman ordered me back to the hotel, where I had the choice of spending the afternoon in the lounge with old ducks having their afternoon fill of tea and gossip, or in our third-floor room with its reek of old air, gin, and vomit. I stayed in the lounge where an old lady taught me how to play patience. I still play it every day; it's a good game for an alone person, like me. Mrs. Duncan, who likes to spy on me, stays in her own room when she thinks I'm settled with my cards. I've always read a lot, too. Books are my companions, my teachers. They tell me things people don't.

I told Tom my drowning story the first time he wanted to take the children to the seaside and I objected. He insisted we go, but even he couldn't make me get in. He tried to pull me in the first day, grabbed my arm so hard it bruised, but my frantic shrieks brought all kinds of unwelcome attention from people on the beach, so he had to stop. He sat on the beach all day every day watching the children and sulking, hardly speaking to me. "You're a real wet blanket," was about all he said. We spent our summer holidays in France or Spain as soon as we could afford it, and stayed well away from large bodies of water. He enjoyed fancy restaurants and bars, but it wasn't much fun for the children, who spent their time whining and demanding all kinds of silly toys and gadgets. Tom always gave in as though he could buy their happiness and affection. As soon as the children were old enough to go away with friends, they always went to a hot seaside resort and came back brown and happy. They found my anxiety about swimming a constant irritant and it became yet another cause for resentment. And then this pool. Tom pushed my fear aside along with other things that didn't matter.

He's concentrating on his tea, making no effort to chat. Is he thinking about her? Well, I don't feel like engaging in small talk, anyway. I'd better eat my bun or he'll think me ungracious.

Mousetrap

Many things have scared me. Daddy often worked at home. I walked into his study once after he'd said we weren't to disturb him because he had to give a lot of dictation. Mummy was out shopping and I'd cut my finger using a knife I wasn't allowed to touch. I knew I'd get into trouble, so I avoided disturbing him as long as I could, but the bleeding wouldn't stop and I thought I'd bleed to death. I found Daphne sitting on his lap and they were kissing, their faces disgustingly mashed together. Daddy's face turned a shocking shade of purple when he noticed me. "Daphne's straightening my tie," he said in a grating tone that showed he didn't like me any more. "Get out and keep your mouth shut!"

Confused, and I puzzled over it as I wandered back to the kitchen, dripping a speckled trail of blood crumbs on the cream carpet as I went. Why did she have to sit on his lap and kiss him just to straighten his tie? And besides, on the rare occasions when I sat on his lap I'd sit sidesaddle, and he was never keen on kissing me, even though he liked to caress and fondle me a lot, especially my fried eggs, as he liked to call my breasts. Anyway, I would have hated kissing him because his aftershave made me feel sick. When I screwed up the courage to tell him that once, he slapped my face. I hate aftershave—usually. I knew what he did with Daphne wasn't right, and I knew just as surely that it wasn't something I should talk about to anyone, especially Mummy. After they'd left, I went back to clean up, but could find no trace of the trail. Could that have been my little jackdaw saving me again, pecking up the crumbs? He always comes to me when things have gone badly wrong and I need raising above my troubles. He whispers to me so sweetly. Jackdaws are clever enough to learn our language, and they love to steal pretty shiny things and hide them in their nests.

I stole a brooch from Woolworth's once and hid it inside an old teddy bear. No one ever found out. I loved to take it out at night and watch how the diamonds sparkled in the lamplight. I know they were only cheap glass, but they were magical and real then and didn't lose anything for knowing the difference later. I kept it for years until Tom threw it away. "No wife of mine wears that rubbish!" Next day, he bought me a real one. I sometimes hold that costly brooch up to the light, but there's no thrill in it. I've thought of stealing another sparkly trinket, of course I have, but it's too risky. They're just waiting for an excuse to shut me up, so it's not worth that heady rush, not worth that small suffocating room with its hard narrow bed, swallowing all those dizzying pills, the wobbly signing of lawyerly papers. I wish they'd leave me alone in my thoughts and my house.

It was no surprise when Daddy left us a few months later, but I was scared just the same. He'd never shown much interest in me and neither did Mummy any more. She only cared when her supply of gin ran dry after her month's allowance had. Food came a very poor second in her housekeeping budget. I tried a few sips of gin once because there was no orangeade left and I was sick of tap water. I've never tried it again, even the smell makes me feel sick. My only wonder was that Mummy could down so much of it before throwing up as copiously as I had. Practice makes perfect, I suppose.

Before long, Mummy was taken to hospital after she wouldn't wake up one morning and I called 999. I went to live with Daddy, who didn't want me any more than Daphne did. But they were all right as long as I kept quiet and out of the way. I never asked for much, and when I did, I usually got it. Daddy enrolled me in one of the best private girls' schools around, and they worked us hard. I made sure I got good marks, which pleased him. I heard him bragging to a friend about me being brainy, and that's the only praise I ever got.

I didn't see Mummy often after that, not until a couple of years later when she was close to death and I had to visit every day after school. All those tubes horrified me. She kept telling me she was sorry for being a bad mother and was always wailing about how afraid she was of dying. I didn't feel sorry for her, only disgusted by how she looked and behaved and smelled. I started worrying about my own death, though, how it would be, if there really was something beyond like Miss Ramsey said in Scripture class. I had never been to church, so there was no one to ask. That's the scariest thing of all to a child, having no one to ask.

I didn't feel like going to Mummy's funeral. I said I didn't feel well enough. They put it down to grief.

Is this man ever going to speak? People say I am peculiar, but he takes the prize. He looks as if he's trying to read his tealeaves. Maybe he's planning something. He's not normal. I can stare at my tea, too. God knows there are enough things swirling around my mind. Tom's death seems to have stirred them all up like an eddy of wind in a sand storm.

Tom wanted me, and that was something. I couldn't see it at the time, but he was another person I couldn't ask about important things. He dealt with all the big things himself. "You need looking after," he said by way of a proposal. "We'd better get married. I need some class on my arm to get to the places I want to go. You'll do me proud." Not very romantic, but there he stood, nearly handsome and ready for marriage. And Daddy despised him, which was my main motivation, plus, Tom never wore aftershave. He never once told me he loved me. I just assumed. I assumed a lot of things because I was ready for my own home. I got Tom's home, quite a different thing. I did get my children, and when I was well enough to be alone with them they brought great joy—until they hit their teenage years, but I suppose most parents say that. Tom indulged them too much, and I never seemed to prevail. I've always been so low-spirited.

I have a nervous impulse to pierce the silence that sits between us like a lump of clay. It feels too awkward and I can't help fidgeting. He doesn't fidget. Still as a tombstone.

"My name's Suzanne. What's yours?"

Silence for a few seconds. He is clearly pulling away from some deep line of thought. "John. What did your husband die of?" He looks up, his mouth squeezed tight as if annoyed to be unearthed from his inner life.

"Cancer. Started in his stomach and spread. It went quickly. Merciful."

"For all of you." It came out like an accusation.

"Well, yes, you could say that. I have two children. A son and a daughter, both in their twenties. Do you have children?"

"No, thank God. Who wants a mad mother? Runs in her family. I should have known better. She was what her father called a free spirit, and I found that whimsical quality enchanting at first."

"If you go to look at that painting every day you must still have feelings for her."

"I mourn what could have been, what we didn't have, what I didn't get. I don't miss her. She was a lot of trouble." He fiddles with his spoon, making it knock against the tabletop like a stoned percussionist, all breaks and starts.

"How sad for her not to have anyone miss her."

"Can you tell me honestly you miss your husband? It's not in your face, in your behavior, in the way you hold yourself. All you feel is relief." He takes a little bite out of his bun and worries at it with his front teeth, the way rabbits nibble at our lawn. The rest of his face remains immobile, dissociated.

"You're very cold about her, and yet you hold onto your grief so hard. Are you stuck in a groove, sort of like a needle on a scratched LP?"

Hard anger sparks in his eyes now, turns them lighter, sharper. His hands press down.

"I choose to keep to my routine, but I can free myself whenever I feel like it. I'm alone, so I do as I please. I'm a writer. I like being alone." A cold tone now. The eyes have lost their spark, look glazed over, like those of my beloved cat just as he died. Tom's, too.

"What do you write?"

"Horror and fantasy. I do a great deal of interesting research." A little smirk, hidden unpleasantness. I hope I'm not research.

He drains his cup with a slurp. He's hardly eaten his bun.

"Well, Suzanne, it's been nice talking to you. Perhaps we'll meet at the painting again."

He leaps to his feet and darts out without paying. Not such a gentleman.

"Did you call, ducky?" Ducky. Doesn't she know how annoying she is?

"No, thank you. I was just talking to my friend. I'll pay now."

"Your friend?"

"Yes, the man I was sitting with."

"Oh." She gives me a funny look and removes my cup and plate. She must have taken John's things while I was daydreaming. I suppose it did look odd, both of us sitting here saying next to nothing. She probably thought we were married.

I hope I can find my way back to the Tube. I can always ask someone. I want to be sure he's gone before I venture out. He made my goose pimples prickle. He's not well—in his mind, I mean. Even so, there was a spark. I need the occasional spark. Doesn't everyone?

I wonder what someone of his sort is like in bed. Cold and business-like probably, not that I'll ever find out because I'll never see him again. I like that painting, though. He might be quite rough because there's a lot of anger there. Could be interesting, but I'll definitely give it a miss. Horror and fantasy? Interesting. I know about horror and fantasy. I should get to know him better.

II

My front door has gorgeous stained-glass inserts, but it always seemed like the door to a prison. I love it now I can walk in and out as I like without wondering what sort of mood Tom will be in. It flies open before I'm halfway up the path, and there's Anne, hovering like a harpy. Our neighbor, Jane Hitchcock, peers anxiously over her shoulder.

"Where have you been, Mother? We've been worried sick."

"I wanted to be alone, Anne. I will come and go as I please." I sweep past them both. "Jane, how very nice to see you. Please excuse me. I need to take a nap."

I pause for a moment as I hear Jane twittering and bustling herself into her cardigan and raincoat and out of the house. Anne looked ready for a fight, though, so I'd better go straight on upstairs.

"Stephen left. He got tired of waiting," she calls after me. I answer with a flip of my hand meant to indicate that he can do as he pleases and she can piss off.

"Where's Mrs. Duncan?" I call back.

"I'm here, Mrs. Benson."

I whip back around, startled. People should stop startling me.

"Where's Anne?" Strange she should run off like that.

"Your daughter left a long time ago." Mrs. Duncan's mouth crumples as if she left out her dentures. It makes a lot of lines when she does that. An unattractive habit. Anne was just here, but I won't argue, not this time. She looks ready to pounce.

I've been watching television for hours, but remember none of it. Why am I stuck in the past when I should be planning my future? I can't shake it off. Reading might help me sleep, but what? I want something deeper than my usual romance novels, something to think about now my mind is at peace, or should be. Poetry. I'll buy some tomorrow. Poems about nature and love are calming. I must lay siege to peace, make it show its face.

While I'm in the bookshop, perhaps I'll look for a horror novel written by a John something. There might be a photo on the back cover.

It's grown dark outside, and I'm staring at the ceiling at nothing, not even a crack. No defects in Tom's house. I can't get that woman out of my head. "Woman Seated on a Bench" by Claude Monet, 1874. No name. I'll do some research and find out who she was. I want to see her again, but not him. Not yet, anyway.

I've been lying down for hours. I'll get out of bed and pace a little, quietly, or the Duncan woman will come sniffing around. The floor is freezing, where are my slippers? Tom liked the house cold. I'll turn the heat up, I've never liked the house cold. My slippers are under Tom's side of the bed. He doesn't have a side anymore, not that he ever used it much. They're both mine now, and my slippers are under whichever of my sides I please.

How liberating to march into the hallway and turn that dial. I wish my room had a lock. I'll order one if they'll let me. I pad back to my own big bed. Wait, I wonder if there's a full moon? The crescent moon throws only a faint sheen at my window through the damp mist. No werewolves tonight. It's raining and the wind whips the trees, making them sway like drunken oafs. How lovely to be inside feeling warm and cozy, looking out on that dreariness. Well, I hope it'll warm up soon and be cozy. I'm fed up with waiting for everything I want.

"Mrs. Benson! I thought I heard something. Are you alright?"

Damn woman, she never leaves me alone, I'll have to get rid of her one way or another. A little something in her bedtime brandy perhaps. She thinks I don't know, but I do some snooping when she's busy plotting with Old Snotty downstairs. I'm entitled to know what's going on in my own house, aren't I?

"Mrs. Benson, can you hear me?"

"Yes, yes, Mrs. Duncan, just turning up the heat, I was cold."

"Oh. Would you like some nice hot milk?"

"No, no, thank you, I'm going back to sleep now. Goodnight."

"Just so long as you're sure."

Hell yes, I'm sure. Hot milk topped with puckered skin must have been invented by the gods of the underworld—the perfect antidote to nectar.

I saw something move down there, I know I did. There! A man is standing under the streetlight, his white face turned up to my window. What does he want? Should I call the police? They'll punish me if they come and he's not there any more. They weren't very polite the last time I thought I saw someone lurking. Tom ridiculed me in front of them, too. I always hide my pills, but Tom watched me take them that night and for a few more days. He let it slide after that, as I knew he would. I hate feeling dozy. The Duncan woman never lets anything slide, but I feel quite bright tonight.

I'll just watch him for a while. His shoulders hunch as he puts up an umbrella. Oh, it's blown inside out! He looks up again and waves as he glides into the shadows. He knew I was watching, even though he couldn't actually have seen me. He must have seen the light go on. Surely not John, not a problem already? It looked like him, but John looks like so many people if you can't see his eyes. It could even have been Tom or Daddy if I didn't know better.

I suppose John could have followed me. I didn't pay attention after the first quick glance up and down the street when I left the café. Maybe he fancies me. But maybe he hates me for what I said. I don't mind if it was John. Not really.

I hope it is not Martin again. I wanted to improve my tennis and join the club, get to know people. Never good at tennis at school, I was still hopeless, although Martin was very patient. When I said I was quitting he got really angry. We'd gone for coffee a couple of times, and lunch once, followed by a quick fuck in the pool house. He asked me to his place for dinner a few days later, claiming he was good at pasta. Tom stayed out all the time, so I could have. Although he was handsome I didn't fancy him that much because he was a clumsy lover, went at it as if he were plowing a field, nothing like darling Patrick. He used sandalwood soap, and I could never make up my mind about that. Subtle, but too much like incense, which always turned my stomach in church. He had bad habits, too. For one thing, he picked his nose when he thought no one was looking. I saw because I am vigilant; I have always known I must always keep a close eye on people, and I'm good at doing it surreptitiously. He stalked me for over a year. The police never found anyone when they came. Their sirens probably frightened him off.

Martin stopped his shenanigans around the time we found out about Tom's cancer. He was my second stalker, and I don't feel like dealing with a third. These affairs always end up being inconvenient. I called him once about the stalking. He said what I expected him to. I was imagining things, he had never been anywhere near me or my house, I was just another crazy rich housewife with not enough to do, and so on. Bastard. I've never known a single person who hasn't betrayed me one way or the other. Sometimes they did wicked things, and sometimes they just buggered off and left me stranded.

Mousetrap

I don't mind too much if was John because I might never see him again otherwise. It won't be so easy to get away to London again.

I must stop visiting the past. This is my future, starting right now. I will get into my bed right now and sleep warm and well and long.

III

"I'm going back to my place, Mother. I have some things to do. You know, you could turn part of this house into a small flat. It could be nice, and I'd be here if you needed anything. You're not getting any younger." Her teeth aggressively and messily mashed the last of her eggs and fried bread. I'm sure I taught her to eat with her mouth closed. She still looks like a teenager.

"What an interesting idea, Anne. You must have been awake half the night thinking that up. I could ruin my—yes, my—house by dividing it; you could live rent-free where you could do whatever you want when you want, have friends around at all hours to a place with a pool and an ever-ready kitchen; you could devote yourself to good works without ever having to resort to an inconvenient job. And you might occasionally be at hand to take care of your doddering mother."

"You have no respect for what I do," she screeched, little fists clenched to her chest. "You haven't an ounce of social responsibility. Daddy would have wanted me to be here doing good things. You're such a bitch!"

"I'll have you know I marched in many ban-the-bomb protests before I got married. On the other hand, your father thought the bomb was a good idea, would keep those commies and wogs at bay, as he put it. Your lifestyle is a rebellion against him. I am not going to make my house into flats, and you won't be living here again. You may visit, yes, but it's important that you telephone first, and you must always let me know where you are. Give me your keys."

I watch her face evolve from brat to hissing cat. Fascinating. She opens her canvas sack, digs for the key chain and makes a great show of disengaging the ring holding the keys to my house. She looks at me for a few seconds, combing her hair with her fingers, moving in slow motion.

"You're completely mad." She throws the keys at my face, grazing my cheek. She moved so fast I didn't see it coming.

"You assault me and I'm mad? Leave my house now and don't return until you are prepared to be respectful. And make sure you ring and tell me where you are."

I hear the key turn almost silently in the front door. Stephen. Anne runs out to him and I hear shrill whispers. Looking around, everything in my shiny white kitchen has gone misty, like it does when I get upset. Even the toaster looks wavy. That child has a lot to answer for.

"Mother, whatever is going on?" Stephen is a pompous twerp sometimes. I never thought a son of mine could turn out like that, I never pictured him tall and broad and solemn.

"Anne wants me to make part of this house into a flat where she can live rent free. She was very rude when I refused. This is my house and I mean to enjoy both it and my privacy. When I asked for her key she threw it at my face." I pointed to my cheek.

"That was a terrible thing to do, Anne!"

"Oh, shut up! And don't pretend it wasn't your idea!"
The cold leaden lump settles back in my stomach. It lifted for a little while. After Tom died I felt light and free until my children came back. They should have warned me they were coming, at least given me some kind of hint.

"Well, Stephen? Is this a grand conspiracy to help yourselves at your earliest opportunity? You are both used to me being weak, always eager to keep the peace, but things have changed."

"Well, it is Dad's money, he earned it, you must admit that. This is a huge house, much more than you need. It can easily be made into three flats."

"Yes, Dad earned it, but so did I, in so many ways I won't go into. And it is not for you to decide how big a house I may or may not need."

"I happen to know Dad thought about doing it. I found the plans." Stephen's tone warbles with indignation. "He clearly meant to provide us with homes here."

"You know nothing. A few years ago your father considered building an even bigger house. That's why he thought of turning this house into rental flats, but the planning people turned him down. You've been prying, Stephen. You have no right to go through your father's papers. I'll have your keys, too."

He yanks them out of his pocket and throws them on the table, tongue-tied and self-pitying.

"Neither of you will ever live in this house, and anyway you haven't lived here for years and years. Why would you both want to return, just like that? Without any warning."

"Anne's right, you have gone mad."

"I forgot to tell you, Grandfather rang yesterday afternoon while you were out. He was sorry he was away and couldn't make it to the funeral." Anne smirked. "He wanted to know how you were bearing up. I said we had no idea where you were. That you'd just disappeared. He was very upset."

"Anne, you could have just told him I was out. Of course he didn't come, he never puts himself out for me, and he never liked your father. I haven't seen him for years. And you'll notice he didn't ring back."

"He was very concerned and asked me to get in touch as soon as I had any news. I rang him after you went upstairs. I asked him why he was so agitated. He told me a very interesting story."

My mind flips a little, I can't quite catch my breath.

"Anne, what are you talking about?" Stephen sounds bewildered and angry. He has never liked uncertainty. I know how he feels.

"How you had to go to a quiet little rest home after your mother died. That was after you ran away and came back a week later, filthy and delirious. You kept gibbering about a man who'd abducted you. And after that you had lots of anxiety attacks because you said he was watching the house, watching you. A man no one else ever saw."

My eyes seem glued shut as I relive that panic, feel that man's breath and hands all over me, smell his days-old sweat, feel his eyes always boring through my bedroom windows after I escaped and made my way home. His name, his name, was it Martin? No, that was the other one. Why can't these dreadful people leave me alone? Why can't anyone leave me in peace, let me rest my mind? Breathe, breathe, find your center, do not go to that mad, deep place.

"Mother?" Patrick sounds worried. I must pull myself together.

"You know your grandfather is very hostile toward me, don't you? Did he ever tell you about the time I caught him fucking Daphne? I was only a child, and he left us for her soon after. Think, Anne, think. Why would a grandfather tell you such a story, even if it were true? Because he's a troublemaker. Do you remember the last Christmas he spent here? The last one because your father banned him from the house after he told you your tits were as luscious as soft sweet melons. I know he was drunk, but still. Think about that, Anne."

Anne's face is a caricature of squeamish horror, probably because her mother said fuck and tits more than anything else. I love shocking people with that language. She'd clearly forgotten her grandfather's slip until now. I always wondered how many other slips he might have made, although I always tried to make sure he never spent time alone with her.

"Don't even think of trying to use the mad card with me, either of you. Now, time to go. I need some peace."

They slouch out, one of them slamming the door hard enough to make its windows rattle. I go to lock up behind them. Already locked. Shit, one of them must still have a key; I'll change the locks again. The only people coming here in future will be invited. I love my children, but it's important I keep them at arms length, keep control of my own destiny. It's essential to keep those children at bay, they always knock me off balance.

I check my face in the cloudy distortion of the antique hall mirror. I can't see any graze, can't feel it when I run my fingers over my face, so she didn't break the skin. I place the keys quietly on the silver platter under the mirror where they have always waited.

The house is quiet, except for the hall grandfather clock, its stormy reflection looming behind me. It's a pretentious mahogany thing, and I hate it. Tom loved it and even wound it on his way out as he left for his last trip to hospital. It took every ounce of his strength and left him out of breath for the whole journey. The thought of that damn thing ticking and chiming on and on seemed to comfort him, as if he believed he would go on as long as the clock did. For me, it counted out the seconds until his death. He implored me to keep it running, but I can't be bothered, although I wound it when Old Snotty drove me home from the hospital the day he died. When it runs down again, that's it. I might give it away. Or sell it.

"Mrs. Benson! Mrs. Benson!" A hard hand shakes my shoulder. I'm painfully stiff from sleeping with my head on the kitchen table. "You were talking in your sleep. A bad dream?"

"No, I'm just tired. You gave me my pills this morning, you know how sleepy they make me. Why did you give me two?"

"You didn't seem well and they keep you steady, Mrs. Benson, keep you steady."

She has got to go.

How sad I parted from my children that way. They got me off kilter.

The doorbell. Damn. I won't answer, I'll just peek from behind the curtain. A man, the same man I saw last night, I think. He has his back to the window, I can't see his face, it could be John. He turns and I see it's Old Snotty, Tom's solicitor, too much paunch and too little hair for John. He's my solicitor now, and I want to sack him. Hell, the Duncan woman opened the door. I compose myself as he enters, trying to look as if I own the place. Which I do.

"Good morning, Mr. Snodgrass. What an unexpected pleasure." Thank God I got the name out, I'm always afraid I'm going to slip up.

"Good morning, Suzanne. How are you bearing up, my dear?" How about calling me Mrs. Benson?

"I'm very well, thank you. Please come in. I'm afraid the house is all sixes and sevens."

He mutters the usual pleasantries.

"I need to acquaint you with the terms of Tom's will. I called round yesterday, but Mrs. Duncan said you'd disappeared. She rang me after your safe return, such a relief." He cocks his head, waiting for an explanation. Nosy old sod.

"I went out for a little peace. Mrs. Duncan is apt to be dramatic. Are there complications?"

"Not in so many words." I don't like the sound of that.

"Your husband left some small bequests, and fifty thousand pounds to each child, to be paid immediately." That should keep them quiet for a while.

"You knew he had instructed me to pay for the final arrangements out of the estate. I trust they were to your liking?" He clutches his briefcase to his chest. No papers to make me sign?

"Yes, a lovely service, thank you." They hadn't even trusted me to make the arrangements myself. Not that I wanted to be bothered with it all, but still. What's the old boy so loathe to tell me?

"Tom felt that you sometimes act, . . . er, impulsively. So, you will not have access to the principal of the monies he left." And on he goes. I will get a monthly allowance, the house must be sold within the year as I don't need such a large space, Mrs. Duncan will be retained at his discretion, and other insulting restrictions. He takes a deep breath and looks at me like a thief looks at the judge.

"I have already sent the boy his bequest and I will hold Anne's until she contacts me." He looks over his glasses at me as if expecting an eruption. Odd he should hold on to Anne's money, but sends out Stephen's. Doesn't he think women can run their own affairs? Stay steady, don't forget it was Snotty who facilitated that little "rest cure" after the Martin episode. Tom has treated me like an idiot who can't manage my own affairs. Betrayed again.

"How big is the estate?"

"Four million pounds, give or take a few thousand. And a couple of commercial rental properties that bring in a good income."

"How big is my allowance? I'll need money right away."

"Three hundred pounds a month. I will take care of all the major expenses, including Mrs. Duncan's salary. And I have begun looking for a smaller house for you." That sideways glance again. He's sweating, I can smell it.

"Stephen found some old plans of Tom's and he and Anne have some idea of dividing the house into flats and living here. I don't want that. I want to stay here on my own. And I hate Mrs. Duncan."

He's adopted the sad droopy look of a bloodhound. "Your children have been gone for a long time, Suzanne. I remember when Tom drew up those plans and they were rejected. Don't worry about that. But you must move to a smaller place with less upkeep. Four million pounds doesn't go as far as you might think in a house like this. Especially with private medical facilities charging what they do."

The children came to the funeral, how could he not notice? Didn't he see them leave just now? Maybe he's getting too old for the job. I'll have to keep my eye on him and sack him if he's senile. Medical facilities? He probably needs a rest cure, but I certainly don't, and I'm not paying for his. I'd better keep an eye on my money.

"I'm perfectly capable of taking care of my own affairs. I'm going to fight this."

"It's airtight, I'm afraid my dear. I know it's hard, but it's for the best. Life is very complicated these days." He emits an absurd melodramatic sigh.

Pompous ass. Will Stephen be as bad at that age? He's backing away. "Thank you, Mr. Snodgrass. I expect to see a copy of the will and a financial statement by the end of the week."

He seems only too glad to scuttle out. I can hear him and Mrs. Duncan muttering together, conspiring.

You son-of-a-bitch, Tom, I hate you. And I wonder what kind of fees old Snotty will get out of this little arrangement. I'll curl up on the sofa for a while and calm myself. They're all against me, including my own husband and children. They all conspire to deprive me of my freedom and property. My life. Have I done nothing to earn respect and love? Nothing?

Think good thoughts, don't let them do you in. Patrick is the best thought, except thinking about him can make me hot and bothered. I hadn't been married more than ten years and was still considered a beauty. I'd started to attend our parish church and he was the new curate. Handsome, educated, a good talker who never seemed to take any notice of his plain wife. I thought him luscious and decided to consult him about a "crisis of faith." I didn't have to do much talking, he never ran short of words. I asked about lust one day, which gave him pause. He offered the standard answer: God's will inside marriage, and so on. I looked him in the eyes and saw his real opinion. Lust was good, lust was present. I went after him, I admit. On what I think of as D-day, I'd been sitting opposite him in a short skirt that showed off my legs—which are still rather good—and I could tell he was thinking about their end-zone. He opened his Bible over his lap in a hurry when he caught me looking. I smiled and said, "I want you, and you want me. Don't you think it would be heavenly?" He was as weak as any other man, for all his sermonizing.

He had a convenient settee in his study that saw a weekly workout from then on, until the Vicar barged in one day. The main business was over, but we were still buttoning up. He glared at me as I crept out, making me feel dirty, and I wanted to kill him for it. Patrick left the parish soon after. I read in the local paper that he'd felt a call to minister to the inner city poor. Banished to Birmingham. I never went back to that church, or any other. I mourned my lost love for over a year. I could hardly get out of bed some days. Tom was harsh and impatient and made me go to the doctor, who prescribed more pills that I didn't take. All I needed was Patrick, the love of my life. Husky, lusty, urbane Patrick.

It's been less than a week since that last hospital visit, seems unreal. Tom looked all white and sterile—his face, the sheets, the walls. Not a hair on his head.

"I knew about that curate. Vicar rang me up. Said you hit him with a brass paperweight. Gave him a concussion. Said you needed help." He paused to gather his ebbing strength. "Said I'd see to it. Sent the church a handsome donation. So angry. Wanted to beat you. Know you needed more, could never get it right. Never knew what to do. Your mind. Always going down into strange places none of us could follow." Tom gasped for breath, he hadn't many more in him. "Find Anne, try to make things right. Wish I could have seen her once more. Took Stephen's death hard. Don't blame her. You stayed so calm, icy. You never looked at her afterwards. Never spoke to her unless you had to. She thought you were sorry it wasn't her."

He panted and coughed like the little engine that couldn't.

"You're imagining things, Tom. Both of them are right here."

"You need help. Rely on Snodgrass. You went right downhill after your father died. Why? Hated each other."

Tom was close to death then and hallucinating most of the time. Anne sat right beside him on the other side of the bed. She looked angry. With me or him? Stephen stood behind me, his sharp fingernails biting into my shoulders, his cold breath on my neck. Old Snotty lurked in a corner.

"There was a woman. She gave me a son. He is provided for. Ian."

"You're dreaming, Tom. It's the stuff they give you for the pain." I said it gently, but was pretty bored with the whole thing by then, and annoyed he mentioned Patrick in front of the children. I'll deny it if they ask. Ian?

Tom looked at me and shook his head.

"I'm sorry. Is it hard to watch me die?"

"No, not really," I said. He looked sad and tired. Very tired. I wished he'd go to sleep and stay asleep, once and for all.

IV

I need to see that painting again, to look into her face, insert myself into her thoughts. I might invite the children over for dinner tomorrow, make my peace. They should be over their sulking by then, it never lasts long. A takeaway Chinese, I think; cooking bores me to death. Anne might turn her nose up, but Stephen will love it. He always loved Chinese food, even when he was so sick he could hardly breathe, let alone swallow. He actually did stop breathing once. I was sitting right by his bed and he gave out this funny gasp and his mouth sagged open. I screamed and breathed life back into him, puffing and puffing as hard as I could. The bastards pulled me off his little body and stuck me with a needle and I woke up in a hospital bed myself. Stephen came back to me though, he hadn't really left. He visited me every night while I was in there, which is more than his father did. I should be nicer to him because I could have lost him. Yes, definitely Chinese.

A faint rustle by my side. I don't turn.

"Hello, John." I love the way my voice sounds so clear and confident.

"Shh!" a female guard hisses. The male guards are much nicer. Perhaps paintings of women calms their nerves.

"Hello, Suzanne," he whispers in my ear. His frigid breath makes me shiver.

"Shh, they'll separate us if we're noisy."

This is a beautiful place, a quiet, good place. They will never look for me here, and I never want to leave. I inhale, reveling in his sharp sweet aroma. My little jackdaw never leaves me now, roosts on my shoulder where he can whisper into my ear, warn me of what's coming.

I must use my silent voice or they'll send me away.

"Did you come to my house that night we met?"

"Of course, Suzanne. I come to you every night, don't I?"

"The painting draws me in, holds me."

"She holds us both, Little Mouse."

About the Author

D. A. Spruzen grew up near London, England, earned an MFA in Creative Writing from Queens University of Charlotte, and teaches writing when she's not seeking her own muse. In another life she was Manager of Publications for a defense contractor. Her short stories and  poems have appeared in many publications, and she is the author of Not One of Us and Lily Takes the Field, the first two books of The Flower Ladies Trilogy. She is currently seeking a good home for her novel, The Blitz Business, which is set in WWII England. She and her husband live in Northern Virginia with a Jack Russell terrier, who doesn't know he's old and doesn't know he's small.